The Holy Well

The Holy Well

Valentin Katayev

Translated from the Russian
by Max Hayward and Harold Shukman

WALKER AND COMPANY
New York

Library of Congress Catalog Card Number: 67–13226

Printed and manufactured in Great Britain

Published simultaneously in Canada by The Ryerson Press, Toronto.

INTRODUCTION

INTRODUCTION

Valentin Katayev belongs to the small pleiade of Soviet writers—others are Ilya Ehrenburg, Konstantin Paustovsky, Leonid Leonov, Venyamin Kaverin and Konstantin Fedin—who made their mark in the twenties, and who have survived to the present day as the remnant of a brilliant and tragic generation. They witnessed the cynical betrayal of the Revolution's early promise, the establishment of a regime which systematically degraded the national culture while pretending to foster it, and the mass murder of the country's finest talents. They were each lucky to survive—as Ehrenburg has said, it was a lottery—during the satanic reign of terror which lasted from the mid-thirties to Stalin's death in 1953 and from which they even saw the War, with its more straightforward horrors, as a merciful release. There are echoes of this period in *The Holy Well*. In the early part of the story the episode involving the great poet, Osip Mandelshtam, whom Stalin destroyed while sadistically trying to put the onus for his death on his best friend, Boris Pasternak, is clearly intended by Katayev as a memorial to his many ill-fated contemporaries. By contrast, there is a vivid reminder of the ugly time-servers who thrived under Stalin in the figure of the 'human woodpecker', Prokhindeikin (the name is derived from a colloquial word for 'scoundrel'). This creature, with his post-Stalin reincarnation, the itinerant 'intellectual', Alfred Parasyuk, (a type still commonly sent abroad, alas, to represent his country), is a superb composite portrait of those who achieved dominance by their ability to fawn and pander. But then, *everybody* had to adapt to circumstances in order to survive, or at least stand a chance of doing so. Everybody had to be a mimic, apt at reproducing current gobbledegook to order. We in the West will never understand the inner agony and the depths of self-contempt which this entailed for Soviet writers, but Katayev has at least produced an adequate symbol in his fantastic 'talking cat' (page 47) which—significantly, in Georgia, Stalin's homeland—dies while being trained to mouth the latest jargon phrase.

Although Katayev made inevitable concessions to the pressures of the day (particularly in some of his work of the post-war period), he never became a 'talking cat' and his work retained a certain romantic flavour, characteristic of the 'Odessa school'—he comes from the same background as Isaac Babel and Konstantin Paustovsky—which saved him from the drabness imposed, at the worst periods, by socialist realism. Furthermore : he shared with his younger brother, who under the pseudonym 'Petrov' collaborated with Ilya Ilf in *The Twelve Chairs* and *The Little Golden Calf*, a gift of humour which he displayed in his early satirical works, *The Embezzlers* (1926) and the play *Squaring the Circle* (1928). Both of these are Soviet classics.

From the early 'thirties, owing as much to the spirit of the times as to extra-literary pressures, his writing took a more serious turn. The satirical side of his talent was overlaid by a lyrical tone in keeping with the orthodox enthusiasms, whether feigned or sincere, of the 'thirties and 'forties. His *Time Advance!* (1932) was one of the most successful novels devoted to the achievements of the first Five Year Plan, and it captures some of the genuine excitement of those comparatively innocent days. In 1936 he published the first part of a historical chronicle, *The Lone White Sail*, which stands out in the wasteland of a literature now seriously handicapped by moral and administrative pressures. It is a fresh and good-humoured story about Odessa during the Revolution of 1905, and it was made into a memorable film (1937). It is one of the very few books from that period which can still be read for pleasure. The fourth part of this chronicle, *For the Power of the Soviets*, deals with underground resistance in occupied Odessa during the last war and, when it first appeared in 1948, it was denounced as a 'political blunder'. The accusations were the same as in the better known case of Alexander Fadeyev's *Young Guard*, namely that war-time resistance had been shown as something for the most part spontaneous (which it indeed was) rather than as a movement carefully planned, organised and directed by the Party and Stalin personally. Like

Fadeyev, who, perhaps partly as a result of his experiences at this period, committed suicide in 1956, Katayev was obliged to rewrite his novel in accordance with official criticism of it. The new, 'corrected', version came out in 1951. It is perhaps the memory of this particular indignity that gives such a painful ring to the nightmarish episode of the 'talking cat' in *The Holy Well*.

The post-Stalin period was for Katayev, as for the other writers of his generation, a time of difficult readjustment which was not just a simple acceptance of political relaxation and the enlarged measure of creative freedom that it brought. Not all of them could bring themselves, like Ilya Ehrenburg, to play an active and conspicuous part by their own writings in the long and bitter campaign for the liberalization of Soviet cultural life. Katayev, Leonov and others evidently found it difficult —and perhaps a trifle undignified—to publish work which appeared to repudiate their own undeniable past and the Stalinist orthodoxy with which, willy-nilly, they had been associated. At the same time, they were left in the shade by the young writers who, untainted and untrammelled by the past, burst on the scene in the 'fifties and 'sixties. Rather than compete with them in the vast work of restoring the values blighted by Stalinism, Katayev modestly contented himself with an ancillary role. As editor of the monthly literary periodical, *Yunost* (Youth), from its foundation in 1955 to his replacement by the more flexible Boris Polevoi in

1962, he was mentor and protector to many of the younger writers, some of whom have explicitly recognised their debt to him. *Yunost*, together with Tvardovsky's *Novy Mir*, has played a crucial part by giving aid and comfort, at a period when they were more vulnerable than at present, to such new talents as the young novelist Vasili Aksyonov (best known for his *Ticket to the Stars*, published in *Yunost* in 1961, which first posed the whole problem of the gulf between the generations), and the uncomfortably experimental Anatoli Gladilin (see page 129), not to mention the poets Evgeni Evtushenko, Bulat Okudzhava, Bella Akhmadulina, among many others who sometimes found refuge in the pages of *Yunost* at moments when it was difficult to publish elsewhere. As a consequence of Katayev's liberal editorial policy, *Yunost* and its young authors were constantly under attack in the fierce literary struggles of the late 'fifties and early 'sixties. Conservative critics often accused the young (and their older sponsors) not only of ideological sins, but also of inferior literary quality. There is an ironical response to these aspersions in the assumption by Katayev (p. 101) of the self-deprecating label *mauvisme* (from the French *mauvais*) for the style which he espoused as editor of *Yunost*.

Now that the great literary battles have subsided somewhat, and *mauvisme* understood as the flouting of 'socialist realist' convention, is tolerated, if not accepted, Katayev has judged it possible, without appearing to

13

join an undignified scramble to the bandwagon, to publish at last a work of his own—his first, except for a belated second part of his historical chronicle, to appear since the death of Stalin.

The Holy Well, published in *Novy Mir* of May 1966, is a highly personal work, containing sometimes obscure allusions to people and events which seem to have a largely private significance, e.g. the tiresome Kozloviches, inescapable bores who pursue the author and his wife even beyond the grave. With its lack of concern for the rules of 'realist' narrative, it looks strange in the general context of traditional Soviet prose. It is best described as a kind of 'search for lost time' conducted in the style of a Fellini film—the influence is indeed explicitly acknowledged in the story itself. The pretext for a long sequence of dream images relating to the author's past and, in particular, to his journey to America in 1962* is the state between life and death brought about by a difficult surgical operation. The device is a self-consciously literary one, as we see at those moments in the story when the author's mind struggles free of its anaesthetic-induced trance to note possible titles for a work based on this dream journey to the past. It is also a good excuse for the creation of a somewhat 'other-worldly' atmosphere which might otherwise be seen as an affront to materialism. It is certainly unusual to find a Soviet story opening

*He was publicly attacked by Khrushchev for having allegedly made 'imprudent remarks' during this journey. What Katayev privately thought about Khrushchev at that time is suggested by his reference on p. 133 to a 'world-famous Russian eccentric'.

with a plausible description of the daily routine in paradise. The air of unreality, the suggestion—again very unusual in a Soviet context—that the mind may not be entirely captive to our familiar co-ordinates of time and space and that it might escape, through dreams or shifts in 'normal' time sequence to visionary states, is underlined by frequent allusions to Pushkin's mystical poem 'The Prophet' :

> Tormented by my spirit's thirst,
> I wandered in a gloomy desert
> And a six-winged seraphim,
> Appeared to me at a crossroads ;
> With fingers light as sleep,
> He touched me on the eyes,
> My eyes, all-knowing, opened wide,
> Like those of a frightened eagle.
> He touched me on the ears,
> And they were filled with sound and tumult,
> And I heard the trembling of the heavens,
> And the flight of angels on high,
> And the movement of monsters in the sea,
> And the growth of the vine in the valley,
> And he bent down to my lips,
> And he tore out my sinful tongue . . .
> I lay, like a corpse in the desert,
> And God's voice called out to me :
> Arise, Prophet, and see and hear . . .

Though this was certainly not intended by Katayev, these lines could well be taken as a parable of the rebirth of Soviet literature which also, for a long time, lay like a corpse in the desert. The publication of *The Holy Well* shows that Soviet writers, as is their business, are now able to explore private worlds in idiosyncratic ways that would once, not many years ago, have been unthinkable. By proceeding from the assumption that nothing in life is certain, and that hopes are more likely to be disappointed than fulfilled, Katayev has moved away from the optimism which characterised his earlier work. He speaks with the voice of considerable experience.

Max Hayward

The Holy Well

'TAKE IT with a drink of water. That's right. Now sleep well. You'll have heavenly dreams, I promise you.' *anaesthetic & pain killer for operation*

'In colour?'

'Any kind you like,' she said, leaving the ward. Then the dreams began.

We were sitting on a plain unpainted wooden bench, grey with age, under an old tree somewhere at the back of our station. It was beside the holy well from which a thin trickle of spring water ran along a metal pipe into a very small, round pond, a quarter of it overgrown with rushes which had the usual elegance of marsh plants.

A pine tree stood near-by; it was quite unlike the other pines that grow in our woods—thin as masts, crowding each other and reaching up in search of space and light. This one was free, lonely and beautiful in its independence, its thick trunk dividing, lyre-shaped, into scaly, pink branches, its needles almost black. Altogether, the landscape had something delicately picturesque about it—the toy pond, which brief showers of warm rain turned into carefully stitched bead-embroidery, the four small curling clouds crawling like white snails along the blue-lined sky, each at its own height and speed, but all moving in the same direction; particularly picturesque was the figure of the old man who had come to the holy well to wash

19

his bottles.

He took them one by one out of a sack, rinsed them and stood them in a row to dry, before taking them to the station grocery. There were bottles of every conceivable sort ; white and green, bottles for vermouth, zubrovka, port, Stolichnaya and Moscow vodka, Riesling, Georgian 'Abrau cabernet', *tvishi*, *mukuzani* and many other wines—the diminutive half-pint bottles standing with the rest like children among beggars. The old man rinsed each of them carefully inside and out and then stood one beside the other, the row growing longer and longer and yet the sack, we noticed, always remaining as full as before—this bothered us a little, like a simple trick you can't understand.

My wife shrugged her shoulders and said it wasn't a sack at all but a perfectly ordinary bottomless pit, like the bottomless pit of time, in other words—eternity.

Eternity turned out to be not in the least frightening and much more understandable than we had expected. Over the pond, we noticed a small steep semicircular bridge which, together with its reflection, looked like an ornamented capital 'O', and on it stood another old man, or perhaps it was the same one, but with a thin, very long white beard and still thinner moustaches, narrow as shoe-laces. His silk robe was of poor quality; the funnel shape and bright-orange colour of his hat recalled the inverted top of the common chanterelle mushroom. In his wrinkled hands he held, at the level of his knees, a crystal bowl in which a goggle-eyed nasturtium-coloured goldfish swam around. With ceremonial politeness he offered to sell it to us for our dinner but, as he spoke in one of the obscure dialects of South China, we silently walked past; he stood for a long time nodding after us—the head on his slender porcelain neck was not so old after all. Then yet another old man—the third!—appeared walking along the horizon; from a yoke over his shoulder hung two flat wicker baskets which made him look like a pair of scales.

Disturbed by the number of old men—most of all by the human scales—we quickly decided to move from this delightful neighbourhood, reminiscent of the outskirts of Kunming, the city of eternal spring, to some other place, perhaps somewhere in Western Europe.

The old man, it should be noted, still went on rinsing his bottles. In the musical gurgle of the water I thought I heard voices raised in argument.

'Hello. How are you feeling?'

I was mentally prepared for anything, so I was not too frightened.

I liked his narrow, almost boyish face and the dark, gentle hypnotist's eyes which looked at me gravely, as through the slits of a mask. So lightly that I scarcely felt it, he touched my arms at the bends of the elbows, where the blue veins showed through faintly.

'See you tomorrow', he said.

'Tomorrow is only another name for today,' I

remarked, quoting someone else.

But either he didn't like my over subtle joke, or he didn't see the point, for he said nothing and somehow disappeared without my noticing.

Thus began the era of great transformations, as Goethe said on his deathbed.

Holy Well is the name of a small spring near the Station of Peredelkino on the Kiev Railway, where I sat planning this book and thinking about my life.

At first we were not at all bored. We loved each other again, but now this love was rather like a mirror image of our previous earthly love : it was silent and passionless. We had taken a house to suit our taste. It was a small but not too small gingerbread cottage of two stories with a steep tiled roof and a wonderful little garden full of flowers. In front of it, at least five times as high as the house itself, was a horse-chestnut which was always in blossom. In order to see the whole tree from top to bottom one had to go back about a hundred yards, otherwise one got dizzy, and then the house seemed quite tiny, just like a doll's house. Its blossoms were like little wax Christmas trees which had been planted in a set order round the crown of the chestnut, itself composed of large multifoil leaves which looked as though they had been carefully drawn by the delicate brush of an English pre-Raphaelite such as Aubrey Beardsley. The trunk of the tree was almost black, which only brought out even more the waxy pinkish colour of the flowers and the translucent green of the leaves.

22

I am able to describe all this in such detail because my eyesight had become completely normal again—it was ages since I'd worn glasses, and I could see very clearly and for great distances, just as in my youth when I was able to find the range of a gun without binoculars.

Next to the house, as was right and proper if one was dreaming in colour, there were a few bushes of fine lilac with remarkably large and beautiful flowers. We never got tired of admiring its different shades of colour—violet, almost dark blue, or a purple pink. The clusters of flowers were as light as air and yet at the same time so palpably material and solid that you wanted to take hold of them and feel them like bunches of grapes or even like samples of some remarkable new kind of building material.

All around, behind a low wall of fiery red brick, in which every brick was followed by an empty space, there were masses of honeysuckle, well pruned hawthorn and some other beautifully decadent vegetation such as monkey-puzzle trees or philodendrons. In the middle of a smooth lawn there was a sun-dial, to which, however, nobody paid any attention. Nobody disturbed us. We lived just as we pleased, each of us in accordance with his taste. For example, taking advantage of the fact that I was well over the retiring age, I tried to do nothing at all. But my wife liked to cook on an electric grill, making light and remarkably tasty meals out of marvellously fresh and varied produce packed in cellophane, such as fricassée of birds of paradise, and synthetic dumplings. We also ate a lot of wholesome green stuff like lettuce, artichokes and asparagus, and we drank black coffee. We no longer had to keep to a diet, but we avoided heavy food which here was somehow unappetising. We almost fainted at the very thought of jellied pigs' trotters or cabbage soup with yellow fat floating in it. We feasted on large, sweet and always fresh strawberries with sugar and cream, and at sundown we liked a cup of very strong, almost black Indian tea with sugar and a drop of milk. It filled the room with a wonderful fragrance. What is more, I liked to sip chilled white wine, my partiality for which no longer affected my health or made me drunk, but simply gave me a pleasure for which I did not later have to pay. We were also fond of soft cheese which we spread on crunchy hunks of bread undoubtedly baked by angels. I should also mention that we breakfasted on rolls, butter and jam which in its small glass jars looked like some green ointment or hair-dressing.

The weather was very good and bracing, it was almost always sunny, warm and mild, and the damp earth smelled of spring.

Nearly every day we got into a small car and sped along the highway past the strange artistry of road signs. Though they looked like the work of abstract painters they had nothing to do with art, but simply controlled our movements, warning us and letting us know in the symbolic language of their broken lines, zig-zags, triangles, multi-coloured circles, lines and squiggles, about everything that lay in wait for us ahead, that is, in the immediate future. Courbet used to say : 'That which we cannot see, the nonexistent and the abstract, does not belong to the realm of art.' This is true, but it does belong to a realm of some kind, I believe—to a new, fourth realm of a system of signals which is taking the place of the old one. 'Only writing and sound,' says John Bernal, thus debarring colour, 'embody human thought, and now computer systems can give completely new material shape to human thought, to a certain extent replacing language and even going further than language in their development.'

We careered past posters painted in luminous colours, and now and then entered green tunnels of elms, which mingled their remote crowns above us.

Signals from the future rushed towards us, warning us and warding off dangers that lay in wait at every turn of time.

Pillars in black, white, and red glimmered at the bends, and made one think of abstract versions of storks standing alongside the road.

My shoulder no longer hurt. I was never dizzy, and my neck didn't trouble me any more.

My wife was also free of pain. We hardly ever slept, day or night, but mostly sat in old-fashioned armchairs in front of the fire, where a huge log, placed crossways, lay smouldering. She knitted, and I tried to do nothing. Not even to think. I simply looked out of the window and gathered random impressions, all of them without value, scientific, artistic or philosophical. For instance, I observed that two totally different plants could grow out of the same soil, almost out of the very same spot, one of them beautiful and precious, such as a horse-chestnut, the other ugly and cheap, and its wood of poor quality, such as an alder. On the whole I paid a lot of attention to matter, in one form or another. I came to the conclusion that it is not only content that determines form, but something else as well. By observing nature I came to the conclusion that since all we ever see are physical bodies which possess volume—the body of a road, the body of a maple-leaf, the numerous little bodies of sand (for each grain of sand is a body), even the body of mist—painting as such does not exist, and is always a more or less successful imitation of sculpture.

So instead of pictures, there ought to be painted sculpture, and roads ought to stand at the edge of woods, wound on enormous reels, like those used for electric cable.

Even a very beautiful sunset among the trees and the bell-towers, besides colour, had form, volume, weight, as though it had been cast in plaster of Paris and decorated by some second-rate landscape painter.

Once upon a time my wife and I had promised to love each other until death, and even beyond it. It now turned out to be much simpler than we had then imagined, though our love had assumed another form.

Over my sweater I wore a shabby, comfortable jacket, and solid shoes. Just as before, my wife still wore something woollen and grey, and in her ears were tiny diamond earrings, as yet untransformed into pure carbon and brightly sparkling with colours from violet to green. We would often go for walks, and then she would put on a short leather coat and red gloves.

Once, while we were out walking, we met Giulietta Masina with a short umbrella under her arm and we greeted her. She did not recognise us, but she gave a friendly smile. Another time we saw an old man in a straw hat who stood aside for us and then watched us *lafkaesque* for a long time through old-fashioned Chekhovian pince-nez, his eyes full of tears. But it was only when he was hidden from view that I realised it was my father.

Another time we looked at an old watermill, its stationary wheel green-bearded with a thin trickle of water running off it. In front of the mill stood old lumpish willows, like warriors' clubs, with bare twigs sticking out on all sides, suggesting the arrows with which St. Sebastian was martyred. We especially admired the foliage of distant groves. They were mist-blue, with large clusters of rippling trees, probably beeches, which were softly rounded, like painted clouds. The fields of barley had sprouted ears and, as though seen through binoculars, each heavily faceted, well painted ear was distinctly visible. Bright yellow strips of charlock lay on the fields, bringing out the slightest fold in the terrain. On the horizon a Gothic belfry seemed to grow straight out of the ground, and the iron weathercock on top of its cross could clearly be seen with the naked eye.

But the landscape became especially sculptured

when in the distance there appeared a bright scarlet spot, sharp, flashing, gradually growing and turning into the capacious body of a young dairy-maid on her white motor scooter with silver milk-cans behind. She wore her straw-coloured hair high and it went very well with the bright scarlet dress, which revealed without words that the girl was exactly nineteen; for I had noticed a long time ago that blondes of eighteen mostly wear blue, while at twenty they wear black, with a gold belt. She was gnawing at a long cob of maize. From the distance you would have thought she was playing the flute.

Whenever we passed farms with their rich smell of manure and new milk, and little towns with their billiard halls open at night, the road seemed to turn into a main street, with children running about, lovers strolling with arms about each other, and entire, well-mannered families on their way to visit grandmother and grandfather, carrying narcissi wrapped in tissue paper, while in the church thin sabbath bells rang and in the opening of the stone Gothic doorway, which always reminded me of the mark made by a hot flat-iron, wax candles blazed like golden bonfires. We bowed to everyone and everyone answered with friendly smiles, though nobody knew us. It was all very nice, but infinitely depressing.

'You know, I miss our grand-daughter terribly,' my wife said suddenly.

I was amazed, because I had got used to the idea that we had finished with that sort of thing. I myself never thought about the past at all. I had forgiven and forgotten everything. My wife's words came as a rude reminder of the past. I began to imagine the small hands of a child, strong and swarthy, like a gypsy's, with dirty little finger-nails. They reached out towards me, and at once I felt a passionate desire to see my grand-daughter, to pull her up on to my knees, to hug her, to rock her, to tickle her, and to smell her child's body, to kiss her eyes, small, searching, mischievous like a sparrow's, eyes that have just begun to explore the world. I remembered that she was called Valentinochka. It was very easy to see her. I could already see her in my mind, but there were complications, such as her nanny. Valentinochka could not of course come here alone without her nanny. The nanny had to come too.

I said, 'Suppose the nanny does come. So what? But the child shouldn't be separated from her mother.'

'Especially as she is our daughter, after all', my wife said with reproach. 'Have you really forgotten our children? We did have children, you know.' She started to cry. 'Don't you remember? They were wonderful children. A girl and a boy.'

I smiled.

'Yes, yes. Don't cry. Two marvellous children. I can even remember the funny names I used to call them— Jackal and Hyena. Not very fair on them, but amusing.'

'I love them so much', my wife said, her face shining through her tears. 'I love them more than anything else in the world.'

'Even more than Valentinochka?' I asked slyly.

'Of course!'

'Yet there's a theory that grandmothers love their grandchildren much more than their own children.'

'Rubbish! I never, never, never loved anyone as much as my children.'

'But you mean you loved me less?' I replied.

'I never loved you.'

She resolutely wiped her eyes with a scented handkerchief.

'But I adored them. My darling Jackal and Hyena. Do you remember?' she asked.

And I realized she was thinking of a particular day, the image of which was eternally fixed in my mind's eye. It never ceased to stir me, so sharp were its colours, and its dark outline, though somewhat funereal, was brightly lit by a silver sun.

It is difficult to say what time of the year it was. And did it really happen? And if it did, then in what dimension? Such over-sharp shadows and over-bright colours could mean that it was spring or the height of autumn, but judging by the thirst which tormented us all, and the heat and dust, it must have been summer, the very zenith of July with all the city smells of gasoline, road-works, liquid tar, lime, cheap paint made from awful synthetic linseed oil which could poison you or drive you mad with its pungent fumes. Yes, now I remember. It was in fact summer and we were cruising in our scorching old car around the kolkhoz market, near the Kiev station in Moscow, hitting holes in the ground, finding our way barred by road-works, lurching over ruts in the road, skidding on sand or leaving tyre-prints in the newly laid steaming asphalt. Faded red bunting with white inscriptions hung everywhere and the fronts of the houses were festooned with faintly glowing electric bulbs which had obviously been left on by mistake. They added to the glare of the already scorching day and drove one to distraction.

We constantly had to stop, reverse, drive up on to the sidewalk, and turn round. We were forever finding ourselves in another impossible situation. But the inevitable plaster statue or bust of Stalin would appear before us—in the window of a bread store, draped with bunting which had been bleached white by an infernal sun, too much even for the garlands of rolls and plaited bread hanging overhead like strange fossils.

The rear window of the car was piled up with shopping-bags full of tired green vegetables, tomatoes, and wrinkled blue egg-plants, so that now I am sure that it took place at the end of the summer. We had already been to the kolkhoz market and were now driving around looking for a filling station. All around us the ancient shacks of pre-revolutionary Dorogomilov huddled beneath new multi-storey blocks still not plastered but already shabby. They had cluttered balconies and flat roofs, Doric, Ionic and Corinthian columns which blocked the light from the already minute windows. There were Egyptian obelisks at the edges of the roof, and the pseudo-classical sculptures were in a bastard Empire style. It could drive you mad, like the smell of the synthetic linseed oil.

My wife, half dead from the heat, and laden with shopping, sat behind, while I sat next to the driver. The children, Jackal and Hyena, also sat behind with their paws and chins resting on the back of my seat which was covered with faded cloth. The girl was then eleven and the boy was nine, and as a joke I called them Jackal and Hyena. On rare occasions, when they were particularly bad or fought each other, they really were a jackal and a hyena. But by and large we had little to complain of.

Marvellous children. We missed them so much!

Not long before, the girl had been ill with typhus and her hair had not yet grown again. This spoilt her rather pretty face. The boy still had the short fringe of a young school-boy and he had visibly grown out of his jacket. The girl stared gloomily in front of her, assailed by hidden feelings of dissatisfaction, while the boy still took in his surroundings with greedy and even delighted curiosity, so that in his small, weak-sighted eyes the world was mirrored as an ideal and perfect miniature. The girl was not yet as old as Juliet but was bigger than Becky Thatcher. She dressed dowdily, buried herself in books, thought about the meaning of life and, to our knowledge, had already had two or three dates. Her little heart was suffering torments which were not at all clear to me. She was diabolically stubborn and utterly rejected reality, which she showed plainly by turning up her freckled little nose and pursing her lips, stained in one place by purple school ink. The boy had reached the age when he no longer tormented cats, and instead ruined reams of writing paper first with drawings of air battles, burning aeroplanes with badly drawn swastikas on their wings, or tanks with quite well shaped shells coming out of their guns; and then identical repetitions of the self-same familiar face in profile, with a black moustache and the slit eyes of a hypnotist; and finally monstrous, fantastic scribbles, flashes, and clouds of ash from an atomic explosion, labelled with a multi-coloured sign *Kerosima*. Everything thrilled him. To him the world was a beautiful place, full of pleasant surprises. Greedily he stared out in front, taking stock of everything and waiting for any opportunity to express his delight.

'Look,' he shouted suddenly with joy. 'They're selling kvas! Super!'

True enough, in the distance at the end of the street you could make out a yellow tank surrounded by a crowd.

The girl also looked and shrugged with contempt.

'It's not kvas at all, it's kerosene,' she said.

'It's kvas, it's kvas,' the boy shouted with joy and good humour.

'Kerosene,' the girl would not be gainsaid.

It might well have been kerosene, which was sold in tanks like this, but on this occasion it was in fact kvas.

'It's kvas, I can see it,' said the boy.

'Kerosene,' she answered.

'Kvas.'

33

'And I say kerosene.'

They were on the point of turning into a jackal and a hyena when the car got close enough for us to see the tank and the people around it holding large glasses.

'I told you it was kvas,' said the boy with satisfaction.

'It's not kvas, it's kerosene,' the girl hissed. Her eyes narrowed spitefully and her lips blenched.

The car stopped.

'Do you remember that awful day?' my wife asked. 'Do you remember that dreadful yellow tank?'

The word '*Kvas*' had been painted on it in huge gold Slavonic letters.

In a relatively white overall and a traditional head-dress, with her sleeves rolled up, wiping her forehead every so often with a special cloth, a Russian beauty—she looked like Queen Nesmeyana—rinsed thick litre and half-litre jugs, and held them under the tap, from which gushed a foamy brown stream.

'Told you it was kvas,' the boy said generously and with a conciliatory smile.

'Kerosene,' she spat out and turned away.

Standing next to our car was a tall man in wide trousers and pale-blue sandals, and a good quality navy-blue velour hat imported from Czechoslovakia, which sat high and firm on his head, and rested on his thick ears. He was thirstily drinking the noble drink out of a litre jug. The spectacle was so captivating that Jackal and Hyena began to fidget. They got out of the car, fished money out of their pockets, joined the queue, drank a whole litre, which puffed out their stomachs, then climbed back into their seats and put their sticky paws and chins on the top of the front seats. We drove on, admiring the iron girders of the university, which was under construction and was visible from Poklonnaya Hill, not far from the famous Kutuzov shack.

'Well?' the boy asked triumphantly, 'Who was right?'

'It was kerosene', she replied, haughtily sticking up her chin, on which glistened drops of kvas.

We had hardly been able to stand the airlessness, and the dreadful, indescribable heat, which seemed as though it might have come from Hiroshima. It had even felt as though our clothes were beginning to scorch. But our only feeling now, in looking back on it, was one of nostalgia.

'Still, I never loved you,' she repeated, again starting to cry, and through her tears she was the first to see Valentinochka, who appeared with her astonished nanny.

But Valentinochka paid us not the slightest notice. She ran off straight away along the stone path of crazy paving, which had young grass showing green between the slabs. She ran into a little garden, crept into a shed, where we kept our garden tools in great order, and out of it she dragged some enormous old gardener's clogs, which she tried on there and then. Then she got on a tricycle and pedalled off.

Next appeared our son, 'Jackal', who was now a

graduate student. He was wearing old, very tight blue jeans, glasses, a corduroy jacket and worn out sneakers, which were proof of his belonging to the new generation of angry young men.

'My God,' I thought, 'is he going to throw his things on the floor of his room even here, and put those sneakers on his desk, already littered with cigarette butts?' All the same, my heart trembled with love and went out to this lanky, terribly thin young man, our son, whom my wife and I used to bath together: I held him, warm and slippery on my arm, while my wife poured water on to him from a basin, and the two of us, smiling with joy, repeated:

'Water off a goose, water off a goose, wash away your skinniness.'

In fact he was a plump baby, and the skinniness was to come only later.

'Greetings, parents,' he said. He stretched out his neck and touched my cheek with the face of an almost grown man, who does not yet shave every day. 'How's life?'

'All right,' I replied with a feeling of love for him which made my head spin, as in those days when I used to take spasmalgin.

Our daughter, our 'Hyena,' appeared. She worked as a translator. Her auburn hair was done up high, she was lively, cheerful and pretty, and her narrow eyes gleamed with a doped look.

'Hello, Pa, hello, Ma,' she said in a clear soprano, and she kissed us one after the other with the expression

36

on her face of a perfectly dutiful, virtuous young woman.

I always enjoyed kissing her soft warm cheeks and slender neck and I loved to plunge my fingers into her crown of thick, wavy auburn hair, which was back-combed in the current fashion. Then, without more ado, she lay down on the divan, stretching and crossing her straight legs in their nylon stockings. She began to read a book she had been carrying, looking every now and again at a dictionary. I noticed some of the pages were scorched at the corners. It was a new Soviet novel, by an author I didn't know, which she had to translate urgently into English.

Oleg, her husband, also appeared. But before he came into the room I heard his voice. He was in the garden talking to his daughter, my grand-daughter. He had picked her up and she was pushing him away with her fingers spread out, wriggling like an eel and jerking her legs, because he had stopped her climbing on the fence, along which there grew espalier pear-trees, their low branches like candelabra. I put on a sweater, went out of the house and started to take the child away from Oleg. He took hold of her bare legs, while I held her little hands, and we each pulled her in opposite directions like a Christmas cracker made of crêpe paper. We swung her like a hammock and laughed with joy when she began to kick and her mischievous sparrow's eyes sparkled with the thrill of opposition. My God, how I loved that naughty little girl with her swarthy little body, which looked as though it had been slightly smoked, and her auburn hair, that dearest, adorable daughter of my daughter. Her legs were covered with cuts and scratches, old and new.

A warm shower fell, but it was so light and brief that we did not even notice it. As always, at seven o'clock we sat down to eat. Now, of course, I was able to eat whatever I liked, but out of habit I limited myself to buckwheat, cream cheese, and a mug of buttermilk.

My son had, needless to say, already disappeared into thin air, and we had supper without him. I went upstairs to his room where, seeing that his socks, pants, braces, trousers, and the rest were all thrown on the floor and that his sneakers were standing on his desk, I realised that everything was as it should be : he had changed for his evening's jaunt. After supper I went out into the garden and saw him on the other side of the fence. He was on his motor-scooter and behind him, her bare arms around him, there sat, gracious and lady-like, the young milkmaid in the red dress, and they raced along the road into the distance, where all one could see were their neon-lit contours, and the flat oval roof of the filling-station where a blazing 'ESSO' sign glowed like a transparent slab of artificial ice. Long cars sped along the highway into the night, the reflection of neon signs gleaming on their paintwork.

What shall we call it? 'After death.'

'Don't you think things are getting rather disturbed in this house?' I asked my wife that evening.

'Why, don't you like it?'

'Yes, I like it . . .'

'What's wrong, then?'

'Nothing.'

'But what is it?'

'You know, I think they've triggered off all sorts of unwanted recollections, painful associations, things that have already been dreamt. I'm afraid I might dream about that talking cat again, or something even worse.'

My fears were justified. The infection had already reached my blood and my brain. That very night I had a long sweet dream about Osip Mandelshtam running along the lamplit Tver Boulevard in the rain, past a wet, iron Pushkin, his hat on the back of his head. He was chasing after the carriage in which Olesha and I were carrying off Nadyusha. Nadyusha was Mandelshtam's wife: Nadezhda Yakovlevna. We were taking her to the corner of Maroseika and Pokrovsky to a bar, near the Magic Dreams cinema, where there was a gypsy show on the first floor. We called this going to *écouter la Bohémienne*. We sat on each side of Nadyusha holding her hands, so that she could not jump out of the cab like an idiot, and she laughed and struggled to get away, cackled and shrieked into the night, 'Osip, they're ravishing me!'

Mandelshtam ran after the cab and called in a childish, petulant, somewhat nasal voice:

'Nadyusya, Nadyusya . . . Wait! Take me too. I want to *écouter* as well.'

But he didn't catch up with us and instead of going to the corner of Maroseika and Pokrovsky, we went for some reason to a Georgian restaurant, which was on the site, not of the present Aragvi, nor even where, before the Aragvi, the Alazan was situated, but, just imagine, it was in the house on Great Dmitrovka, now Pushkin Street, where today the service entrance to the Children's Theatre stands. This may seem quite improbable, but it is nonetheless a historical fact, and this Georgian restaurant was owned by a private individual, since it was the height of NEP. But that was a minor detail. The important thing was that it was raining and that we got Nadyusha up to the second floor to a private room—an incredibly dismal and badly lit room, without any furniture and looking just like the waiting room of a dogs' clinic. We ordered a bottle of *teliani* and it arrived together with a wet and excited Mandelshtam who had chased after us. He immediately began reciting his latest verses in a high-pitched but insistent lisp (as Batyushkov recited to Delvig). It was something like this:

I shall rush through the encampment of the dark street,
Behind a bird-cherry branch in a black sprung carriage,
Behind a hood of snow, behind the eternal noise of the mill.

And so on. You can check it in Mandelshtam's book, if you can get hold of it (that's exactly what I dreamt: 'if you can get hold of it'.) But meanwhile the

Mandelshtam of my old dream sat down to drink his *teliani*. He recalled a land of mountains, and in a loud lisping voice slyly and haughtily, almost as proudly as Lucifer, began to declaim about a city on a turbulent mountain river, a city famed for its carpets, and about a certain little Caucasian tavern 'where there was wine and good pilaf':

> And the red-cheeked owner there
> Hands the glasses to his guests
> And is always at your service.
> And the strong Kakhetian wine
> Is good to drink in the cellar—
> There in the cool, there in the quiet
> Drink twice your fill, drink together.
> You cannot drink alone.

His plea had no practical purpose, since we were a foursome and none of us had to drink on his own. But one of us had to pay! Then followed these enchanting truisms:

> A man can be old
> But a ram must be young.

> And under a lean moon
> With a rosy haze of wine
> The shashlyk smoke will rise.

To tell you the truth, I didn't dream this at all, it actually happened, but all so painfully long ago that it came to me now in the form of a distant, occasionally recurring dream that would carry me back in a rosy haze of wine (and of course under a lean moon) to that same legendary city of carpets, the favourite province of the tetrarchs. And what had once been not quite a dream, but rather a recollection, has now become a genuine dream, remarkable for its closeness to reality. For instance, the snow was quite real and huge flakes fell slowly and majestically, settling on the evergreen leaves of the magnolias. The whole town was coated with warm southern snow. The unaccustomed passers-by slipped and fell like penguins, cars skidded with a frightful screech of brakes, they spun round, even went backwards; the town was in a commotion, its famous mountain was drowned in the soapy water of the winter sky. Like a flock of lapwings the snow swirled over the monument of Shota Rustaveli, and in all directions the sidewalks of the main boulevard were stained by the juicy imprints of new rubber galoshes, and in the shop windows there were pyramids of sickly yellowing Japanese rowan-berries, the only fruit available in that unheard-of winter, since all the citrus trees had died, by the grace of God, and the local authorities were already working out far-reaching plans for smart skating rinks and ski resorts for the workers.

The nice militiamen, with their black moustaches and velvet eyes, stood at the crossroads directing the disorderly fall of the snowflakes, which looked like huge wads of cotton-wool. They shivered in their smart greatcoats and their soft heel-less boots.

We were so depressed by this winter in the sub-tropics that we just wanted to sleep. But who can be

42

sure that I'm not asleep now? That I haven't been sleeping for a long time?

There is nothing more terrible than the boredom of death which slowly, irresistibly slowly begins in sleep and irrevocably continues thereafter throughout eternity.

My God, what is this all about? We were nearly going mad trying to fathom this town and make the people understand us. But just then through the blizzard appeared the outlandish yet painfully familiar figure of the famous poet Romeo Gerolamo: an ordinary Russian fur coat, a warrior's bearing, his deerskin cap glittering regally with snowflakes, his splendid sculptured face like that of a middle-aged Roman legionary, a hoarse guttural voice and the heavy breathing of one who has dined well.

'My friends, don't be so surprised,' he said with the genial smile of eastern hospitality, 'and don't, I beg you, look for mystery, or still less anything out of the Arabian Nights. There's a very simple explanation: they just don't speak Russian.'

Of course, you must have noticed that I said *we* were going mad. I must explain: 'we' means me and another—let's say—person. Actually the strange companion who came with me to that country was a phantom. Like a shadow he never left me but followed a step behind. This most rare cross between a man and a woodpecker, with his bony nose and clownish eyes, was a heavily built swine, a real animal, a buffoon, a timeserver, an arch-racketeer, an informer, a bootlicker, an extortioner and a bribetaker—a monstrous product of those far-off days.

Yet I remembered him as a slim, hard-up young man, with a tiny spark in his breast. My God, how he had gorged himself and grown fat on other people's left-overs, what a slippery, gross, bloated, talentless beast he had become! Had Nikolai Vasilievich Gogol seen him, he would not have written his '*Portrait*', but something a million times more terrifying . . .

The old man at the holy well washed his bottles, and this awful companion of mine poked into everything, sniffing around, ready to snatch any scrap and carry it off grimacing to his stinking lair and bury it the way a dog buries a bone—somewhere in a corner, under the Swedish or Finnish sofa, or under a pouffe which itself had been wheedled or swindled out of somebody.

He was my frequently recurring nightmare, the prelude to the still more frightful dream of the talking cat.

He was always by me, listening to my breathing and quick to take my pulse; he hung around me everywhere, on the streets and on the steep mountain paths of my dreams. From time to time he would stretch his bony bird's beak towards me, showing his nostrils, and peer anxiously into my soul with his putrid eyes as though to ask: 'I don't suppose you know where I might pick up something on the side? Or squeeze a bribe out of some stupid big shot?'

'Hey, did you hear what he said?' he squealed. 'They

don't understand Russian. We mustn't miss out on that. Okay? Do you agree?'

I could have died from the deathly boredom in that exquisite southern country, laden with northern snow.

The celebrated poet bowed extravagantly to a passer-by, showering him with snowflakes from his fur cap with regal magnanimity.

'Who is that gentleman?' my depressing companion asked in alarm. 'Well? Aren't you going to tell me who he is?' He breathed hotly into the face of the celebrated poet and looked beseechingly into his eyes. 'He's a big shot, isn't he? He might even be a member of a government commission? Why didn't you introduce us? Stop him! Introduce us! I beg you! While there's still time. I'll kiss his backside, I'll lick it.'

'Don't get so excited,' said the poet. 'He doesn't deserve such an honour, especially as it's rather cold. He's only a taster at the Wine Trust.'

'Do you hear?' wailed my irksome companion. 'At the Wine Trust! Think of it! We just mustn't let him go. Or we'll be utter imbeciles. Right? Do you agree?'

'All right, if you want to meet him so much,' the poet said gallantly, and he made an imperious gesture, upon which the wine-taster stopped in his tracks as though dazzled by the sun of poetry, and it wasn't an hour before we were the best of friends and sitting in his living room at a table under an enormous orange lampshade and my wretched companion, on tiptoe with excitement, was shoving his nose into the wine taster's neat moustache. Hypnotically his round eyes, with

45

their hideous lifeless glaze, were saying: 'let's have some wine, let's have some wine, give me some, go on.'

'He'll give us something, you'll see', my wretched companion said to me, and he turned back to the wine-taster's moustache. 'He'll let us have something, I promise you,' he whispered to me. 'Two cases of vintage *mtsevane*.'

I lay like a corpse in the desert.

Meanwhile the guests arrived and the party gradually warmed into an oriental feast, with a slight European touch imparted to it by the elegant young *tamada** with his two or three university badges. He didn't try us too much with the traditional toasts, nor insist too stubbornly that we drain the silver-bound ramshorns, and so we slowly got drunk without his help. Time passed and the feast went on and on without flagging. Our hosts, the *tamada* and all the guests, were passionate fans of the local football team, 'Dynamo', and the ladies were fresh as newly blossomed Shiraz roses, or firm moist vegetables picked in the garden at daybreak, all sober, beautiful, rosy-cheeked, with wavy black hair, alabaster bosoms, like angels painted by the brush of Pirosmanishvili.

* Master of ceremonies.

Standing among the green vegetables, fruit and ewe's milk cheese, the bottles on the table were replaced every fifteen minutes, like a guard of honour. The night dragged on without end, and with all my being I sensed the approach of something frightful. I thought it would go on forever, as in hell. But it was not hell, only purgatory.

At 4.42 a.m. the banquet began to dry up, the speeches first became disjointed and then petered out altogether. Powers of resistance failed completely. It was only a step to clinical death, but the *tamada* evidently decided it was not yet time to end the party, and like the experienced master of ceremonies he was, he had at hand a sure means of breathing life into the expiring company.

'Ladies and gentlemen', he said in a completely morning-fresh voice : 'Your attention, please ! You are about to observe a cat, at first sight an ordinary domestic pet. The cat is called Vaska. But don't jump to conclusions. Come here, my beauty. Puss, puss, puss.' The doors opened silently, by themselves, as in an American horror film, and into the room there came, with doom-laden tread, an enormous pale grey cat, a trained domestic animal with narrowed eyes, eternity glinting in their depths, its upright tail like a soft column of smoke swayed by the dark night air of that mysterious mountain land.

The cat—younger brother to the tiger—circled like a gladiator around the banqueting table and stopped next to its master as though about to exclaim :

'Ave, Caesar, morituri te salutant!'

'Now, comrades!' proclaimed our host triumphantly, holding up a finger with a wedding ring on it. 'Wait, comrades. This is no ordinary cat. This is a talking cat. He can talk.'

'Impossible!'

'But still it's a fact. Euripides, come here. Puss, puss, puss.'

The cat narrowed its eyes still more and jumped obediently on to its master's knees.

'Good. Sit.'

The cat sat down like a human being, laid its big, childlike head on the edge of the table and looked around with the beautiful grey-green eyes of a naughty little girl. Its master scratched it behind the ear, and the cat purred as though it were ticklish.

'Your attention,' said the master of ceremonies. 'Fill your glasses.'

'Now he's going to talk,' said its master, 'Don't you believe it? Then I'm going to convince you. Euripides, my friend, say "mama".'

The cat cringed and screwed up its eyes painfully. Its master took its head in both hands, his thumbs together on top, stuck his first fingers expertly into the cat's mouth and stretched it, and a tense and artificial smile appeared on the cat's childish face.

'Speak!' its master ordered.

The cat made a convulsive swallowing motion with its throat, opened its small pink triangular mouth, showing tiny teeth, and suddenly in a forced mechanical

48

voice said, quite distinctly, like a human, in the purest Russian :

'Mama.'

After which its master said : 'Well done,' and threw it on the floor.

'Unbelievable !' said the guests. 'Amazing ! Unbelievable ! Such perfect pronunciation ! What articulation ! What diction ! Just like the Maly Theatre ! Or rather like the Arts !'

In a flash everybody revived and the dying feast took on a new lease of life. But it didn't last long, and in an hour the company's fuel tanks were obviously running down. But the time to go home had evidently not yet arrived, and the host casually remarked that the cat also spoke French.

'Puss, puss, puss !' he called.

The cat took a long time coming, but finally it emerged through the doors which again opened and closed silently by themselves. Desperately slowly the cat went to its master as though it were carrying out some awful duty entailing unbearable torture and humiliation, but which was, alas, as unavoidable as fate. It jumped slowly onto its master's knees and put its chin on the tablecloth which by that time was thoroughly soaked with the finest of local wines. Wincing at the smell of the wine and the sharp aroma of *satsivi* the cat looked at the guests with its somnambulant eyes in mute appeal and again screwed up its face for all it was worth.

'Your attention,' shouted the master of ceremonies.

'Fill your glasses, please.'

'And now,' he said in a business-like way, taking the cat's head in both hands. But this time he put his first fingers into the cat's earholes and hooked his little fingers in some special way in its mouth, stretching it and wrenching it so that it began to look like some kind of weird flower, such as a pink orchid. The cat gave a start, intending to miaow with a heart-rending voice, but instead it uttered loudly and distinctly in perfect French:

'Maman.'

'There you are,' said its master, sweeping the cat onto the floor, whereupon the animal went slowly away to its home with a smile of disgust on its face, knowing that its act was over for the day and that it could get on with the business of catching mice.

'You know, it's sacrilege,' groaned the human woodpecker, following the cat with his putrid eyes as it walked away. His fat neck swelled and he even whimpered from indignation. 'To have such an amazing animal, to put on such a terrific show but only for your guests at a footling little private get-together, without even any big shots around . . .' He clutched his tufted head. 'Good God, if I had a gold-mine of a cat like that I'd teach the little bastard to tell Jewish jokes. I'd make him into a cat comic. If the son-of-a-bitch was mine he'd appear only at the grandest performances. I'd be number one to the local arty types, I might be made a doctor of science, honoris causa. And just imagine what a fantastic thing I could make out of it, what a terrific way to keep in with the right people, it's a chance in a million!'

He began to mope, and let fall a tear, then he perked up and made a vigorous attempt to persuade the host to perform a noble act of oriental hospitality by giving him the talking cat. Nothing came of it because the host had been to college and did not recognise such stupid feudal nonsense as giving your guest whatever he might fancy. However much my miserable companion tried, however much he fussed and shouted and let fall the tenderest utterances, such as 'I know I'm a son-of-a bitch and I'm proud of it! You can look down on me if you like, but just give me your talking cat! I'll make a man out of him! If you like I'll even compose an oratorio in your honour!'—but alas he had no luck. He had met his match.

The only thing that consoled my human woodpecker was the prospect of at least getting a free case or two of fabulous *mtsevane* wine. Now he paid twice the attention to me. He was afraid I might get ill and, God forbid, what was worse, might die. Anything can happen to you in this world.

'I beg you to look after yourself,' he used to whisper to me at night, coming to my bedside while the wintry eastern stars gleamed through the window. 'Remember, the wine's as much yours as mine. It's for both of us. Now you and I are just like one. Remember.'

'All right, I'll remember.'

We were like two convicts, chained to the same iron ball. I was faint and faltered on the way, but my miserable companion pushed me on mercilessly, further and further. He became a disease, he ensconced himself somewhere inside me, in some secret cavity of my guts, or perhaps even lower; he was a painfully swelling tumour, an adenoma of the prostate, forever poisoning my blood which throbbed convulsively and sullenly in my aorta, barely able to make the muscle of my worn-out heart contract.

If only I could have this tumour cut out!

Who was he? He was a modern version of Bulgarin,* the enemy of everything new, and he had the music-hall name of Prokhindeikin.†

Far below, submerged in the endless snowstorm, lay that exquisite country, with all those magnolias, cute little militiamen, the talking cat and the famous poet's fur cap, and we were flying to the capital of our homeland in a passenger plane shuddering with ice on the wings. Death flew along beside us, ready at any moment to upset all our plans. We were over the Suram pass when we were caught in a fantastic, crazy snowstorm and our plane had to feel its way blind through the mountains, expecting any moment to scrape an aluminium wing against a mist-shrouded crag, and to crash to the bottom of a gorge, into a torrent raging between frozen banks.

In the space of an hour we escaped a thousand deaths and when our pilot finally landed his massive machine on a sandy airfield by the turbulent sea, his hands were

* A notorious reactionary writer and informer in the time of Nicolas I.
† The name is derived from the word for a scoundrel.

trembling and sweat was streaming down his exhausted face and ashen lips. We arrived in the capital of our country while it was still light, and there and then we parted. For a long time, thank God. Perhaps forever. But the tormenting dream dragged on and on endlessly, it seemed, although in fact it probably lasted only a fraction of a second, like death. But then no one knows how long death lasts : perhaps a moment, perhaps even less, or perhaps all one's life. Man lives forever and at the same time he is perpetually dying.

No, let's call it: 'rushing to the stars'.

I was always dying and always living, and from time to time I went back to that marvellous land once celebrated in the verse of Osip Mandelshtam.

Naturally, on returning, the first thing I saw at the airport was the fur cap of our classic poet. He towered like a monument even more stately and magnificent than before. We embraced. And according to the historians, we even shed a tear.

'Much water has flowed, *katso*.'

'Yes, a lot, *genatsvale**.'

'How is your miserable friend?' asked the great poet, giving an ever deeper guttural breath after every word,

* Both terms of address in Georgian.

—it always seemed to me like a splendid caesura in the middle of a classical Alexandrian hexameter. 'Is he doing as well as ever? Actually I always thought he'd go far. He's an odd mixture of human woodpecker and domestic animal. And do you know why? Because besides the nerve of a bootlicker and crawler, the Almighty gave him the phenomenal'—here he became splendidly sonorous—'phenomenal ability, the rarest gift of getting himself photographed alongside the "powers that be". The photographers have hardly trained their magical all-seeing eyes on the central figure when up pops, right next to it, that head, so dreadfully familiar that you don't notice it, with the tuft of hair and bony nose—your miserable companion, who has conditioned in himself a reflex that makes him appear, not a second too early or too late, right in the middle of the group, where he stands expertly on tiptoe and makes himself head and shoulders higher than everyone else, even the central figure. Phenomenal!' He gave a throaty sigh. 'I tell you it's phenomenal! To be a pygmy and look like a giant! Let us hope this historical paradox will soon be relegated to eternity. I mean, this kind of thing can't go on . . .'

'And how's the talking cat?' I asked, wishing to drop the unpleasant subject.

'The talking cat?' The poet was surprised. 'I don't know. What talking cat do you have in mind?'

I reminded him.

'Oh, yes, of course. There was a talking cat! Now I remember. He spoke Russian and French. I have lost track of him. But I think I'll be able to give you the latest news of him by tomorrow'.

Again I dreamt long and sweetly about that hump-backed city. We were sitting in a restaurant above a mountain stream which rushed downhill over the stones, like a flock of sheep, wintry and turbid, depressingly dull, leaden and smoky. High above the precipitous misty bank stood the blue silhouette of an ancient castle and a church with a conical tower, and a fat old organ-grinder, perhaps the last on earth, was grinding away at his one-legged street organ, hung with coloured glass beads like an Easter merry-to-round, coaxing out of the decrepit box the piercing, yet heavenly musical sounds of popular waltzes, marches and gavottes from my childhood, and I wept for Osip Mandelshtam and for the gypsies, for my past, for my first love, for all the ships lost at sea, for all those without joy—well, there's a lot a middle-aged man can find to grieve about after his fourth bottle of blood-red 'teliani'. And I got down on my knees and kissed the hairy, brown, infinitely old hands of the organ-grinder, while the great poet comforted me by stroking my dusty and already balding head, the head of a prodigal son, and said, to take my mind off my all too mournful thoughts :

'Don't cry, my friend. It's not worth it. In God's eyes we're all ships lost at sea. Better come back to sad reality. Yesterday you were asking about the fate of that talking cat. I've been making some enquiries. I'm afraid I have some unpleasant news for you : a few

55

years ago the talking cat died during a routine training session. He was unable to pronounce the simple Russian word "neo-colonialism".'

You could call it that: 'a Story about a Talking Cat'.

I awoke in tears, but the world around me had lost its earlier peaceful calm. I was ill at ease the whole of that day.

'What's the matter with you?' my wife asked.

'A lot,' I answered.

'For instance?'

'Well, now that someone has set all my old dreams and nightmares going, and everything around us has changed drastically, well just imagine I'm beginning to feel the absence of the Kozloviches. Frankly, I rather miss them.'

'Well, that's better than the talking cat, at least.' said my wife.

And, lo and behold, in walked the Kozloviches.

'Oh, it's you!' I exclaimed as I scrutinised them. They didn't have any marks of burning and were not in the least changed. He was wearing a slightly music-hall jacket the colour of café au lait, and trousers the colour of chocolat au lait, shoes the colour of crème brûlé, and wine-red woollen socks. The sleeves of his jacket were a fraction shorter than fashion demanded and his shirtcuffs were a fraction longer than they should have been. But it rather suited him. As before, he was deeply florid, with yellow hair combed straight back from his forehead to the back of his head like the famous Russian flier Sergei Utochkin. His teeth shone like ivory. He was good-natured, would eat anything, and spread his hands slightly as he told us the adventures they had had on the way here. As for madame, she was wearing short, tight stretch pants, remarkably suitable for her straight sclerotic legs and knobbly knees. A heavy prehistoric stone with a little hole in the middle dangled on a silver chain over her red jersey blouse. It was frightful to think what would have happened to her if she forgot to take that stone off before jumping into water. She had beautiful child-like eyes and high auburn hair which, with her turned-up nose, gave a complete picture of the mood reflected in her face, tormented as it was by age and by her awareness of her own beauty. The old lady kept on asking for plain cold water which she poured into herself with pleasure as if trying to extinguish the hell-fire which consumed her childish spirit.

As for Kozlovich, he joined me in drinking chilled white wine, which was scented and rather tart, like almonds—not a wine to make you drunk, and quite harmless to your health.

The Kozloviches sat in front of the fire in old-fashioned armchairs, correcting each other on points of detail and chronology, as they recounted the story of how they nearly went to Turkey, Japan, South America and Socialist Poland, and how after all that, their favourite poodle burned to death.

We were overjoyed, like children, listening to their exciting story.

At the point when Kozlovich himself was turning blotchy and beginning to get a bit angry, though he still smiled bravely with all his teeth (they were like piano keys), our dear friend Vyatkin sidled into the room. Rubbing his small, slightly charred hands, as though from cold, and sheepishly giggling, he sat down at the blazing fire and joined us in drinking our chilled other-worldly wine, nibbling cheese with it.

I drew the blinds and suddenly it seemed rather like an evening near Moscow, only there was no television and the phone never rang.

Later that night we settled Vyatkin in the spare room downstairs and took the Kozloviches through the garden to the old Norman barn, where their beds had been made ready for the night. Taking an old carriage lantern that I'd found in the attic we lit their way as they climbed up the narrow creaking staircase, amazed at our ridiculous idea of sending them to bed in a hayloft. My wife and I exchanged amused glances. One after the other, he in front, she behind, the Kozloviches stumbled through a door and suddenly found themselves in a strange dark room, right under the thatched roof where most likely there were fat chickens sleeping on their perches. We explained that it was an ancient Norman barn and that somewhat appeased them. They obediently resigned themselves to their fate.

Then I suddenly switched on the light and the Kozloviches saw that we were in an enormous low room with a sloping ceiling. In the middle of it stood a huge old wooden bed under a gay cotton canopy. The valance had been drawn back, revealing the bed which was made up in the French manner, like an envelope, with fresh linen sheets and a coverlet. The bedside table was ready with a bottle of sweetened water and an ancient Norman prayerbook with a silver cross on its black velvet binding.

Altogether it seemed rather gloomy.

The Kozloviches looked uncomfortable. Perhaps they were afraid of rats. Triumphantly I threw open another door and showed them a magnificent ultra-modern bathroom, with a wash-basin of cobalt-blue porcelain, and a milk-white bath, all lit by a blindingly bright electric light. Carpeted in rough coconut matting, it shone with tiles and nickel, and was hung with downy, scented pink, green and pale-blue towels and sheets. To prove to the Kozloviches that they weren't dreaming, I turned on some taps and out gushed hot and cold water, foamy like beaten egg-white, and filled the room with the symphonic strains of Wagnerian music and the scent of Guerlain soap.

We said good-night to the Kozloviches. 'If you hear a noise outside during the night, don't be afraid. It means the tide is coming in and the English Channel is pouring through the sluice gates, filling the little harbour of Honfleur, where the fishing boats rock sleepily with the picture of the Virgin Mary on their shabby sails. In the morning Denise will bring you petit déjeuner—coffee, croissants, butter and plum jam. But you won't get any fried sausages!'

We left them spellbound.

Madam Kozlovich was especially pleased by all this.

My wife and I went down the staircase into the garden and I blew out the lantern.

Perhaps my naked body was lying in another dimension and under the arc-lights of the operating theatre pale-blue figures were examining my ancient scars, bullet-wounds, shrapnel scars and the marks of various illnesses, wars, and revolutions.

Several unwashed cars, which had arrived during the night, stood on the lawn. One of them seemed familiar.

'I think the Ostapenkos have come,' my wife whispered. 'And they're sleeping in the car.'

They were indeed fast asleep in their half burnt-out car.

'Let's leave them for a bit. Let them sleep,' I said.

She took my arm and we went deep into the dark garden where, beyond the cart-sheds and the wooden privy, there was a broken fence and beyond it from right to left stretched a canal, along which silently, on the same level as the flat land, two unlit motor barges glided. Loaded with very important and very heavy cargo, they were going from Antwerp to the Maas, or perhaps to Mons, or Maastricht, if such a town actually exists.

We walked along the canal, past a Flemish windmill, its motionless sails hung with rigging, like the masts of a frigate; we walked a long time in silence, when suddenly we found ourselves on a stretch of ground which was engulfed in freezing fog, so that we couldn't tell what it was.

'Where have you brought me?' my wife asked anxiously.

I realised immediately that it was an aerodrome, and at our feet I saw the huge hexagonal paving-stones of the runway.

Mesh radio scanners were rotating like dentists' chairs.

'Are you flying off again?' my wife asked resignedly, since she knew that there was nothing else left for me to do.

I said nothing, and looked down at my shoes. They still looked quite decent: black, shiny, well-polished, they went perfectly with my grey suit and nylon socks, which were the deep colour of burnt bone. They were superb shoes with long toes and low solid heels which had to be looked after with special care, because the smallest scratch at once made them look cheap and vulgar. The heels always had to be flawlessly black, without the slightest mark. Then they were quite in place on a trip abroad, with their flaps and cross-straps on the insteps. So my wife had assured me, and I had wholeheartedly fallen in with the idea.

We didn't have time to say good-bye.

She was still standing alone in the middle of the huge deserted aerodrome when I was already putting my watch back two hours and looking at Amsterdam through breaks in the heavy rainclouds. From a height of a few thousand feet you could take Amsterdam for a small carpet, decorated in a geometrical abstract design. There was no rain on the ground and when I left the plane to get the transatlantic flight, my shoes did not suffer at all, rather the opposite : they were so illuminated by the diffused milky lighting of the Amsterdam International Airport that, even alongside all the dazzling luggage and millionaires' shoes, they shone like mirrors. I had no complaints about KLM. Thank God, everything went off all right during the embarkation as well, and even in the enormous passenger plane, among hundreds of pairs of all kinds of shoes, mine were not the worst. They showed up especially well next to the yellow army boots of my neighbour, a sergeant in the American forces in Holland. With time and daily polishing his had gone dark-brown and gleamed like glass, which aroused in me an anxious curiosity as to where the devil they got such marvellous polish for their boots. Or perhaps they didn't use polish but merely dipped their boots into some vitreous liquid to form a thin glaze, to which they then gave extra gloss by means of high-quality boot-brushes of a particular shape and velvets specially designed for the American forces.

The sergeant sat next to me with his feet on the skirting of the partition separating our tourist seats from the toilets and the pilot's cabin. He was a hefty crew-cut fellow of about twenty-five, in khaki denims and an old leather belt as glossy as his boots.

He had a peaceful enough, well-intentioned look, but something about him worried me, some detail of his dress which I couldn't place, an ominous reminder, a signal of general danger. It was a faded little triangle of felt sewn on to one arm of his denims, a scrap of dark purple with ominous red in it, yellow lightning and the word 'Spearhead'.

Perhaps it was the mark of Cain in the nuclear age.

It was then that I realised that this youth was in an atomic unit and, his work now done (or rather not yet done), he was flying home on leave from his base, after washing out his denims and polishing all the leather parts of his equipment to a glass-like sheen.

Or perhaps everything on earth was finished and, like me, he was just a phantom flying over the ocean at that instant?

Still, he had all the signs of a live human being: on his strong peasant's finger he wore a thin wedding ring, more likely silver than gold, but anyway definitely not platinum. It emphasised his solid, positive qualities as a young family man. Maybe he was even a happy father of several healthy children. This distinguished him favourably from his two companions who were flying with us tourist class across the ocean. One of them was in uniform and the other was in civilian clothes, though it was obvious right away that he was a soldier too, perhaps even a rank lower than my neighbour, but without doubt richer. He had already had a bit to drink and as soon as we took off he pulled a squat bottle of Vat 69 out of a narrow pocket, tore off the wrapping, pulled out the cork with his teeth and took a good gulp. He didn't offer it to his companions but took another couple of gulps and then began to flirt with the stewardess. She was as tall as a guardsman, wore a blue cap, and was without a trace of humour—a characteristic which, according to my observations, distinguishes all the tourist class stewardesses on KLM.

The half-drunk atom-soldier in civilian clothes—perhaps his uniform had got burnt somewhere?—just couldn't settle down and take a nap. Apparently his nervous system was shattered and alcohol no longer acted on him as a soporific. He was tormented the whole time by the need for action. He rang for the stewardess and sent her off for a globe. She brought a rubber one from the navigator's cubby-hole and he blew it up through a special nozzle and then began to search drunkenly for North America, trying to trace and measure our course with his fingers. Then he let the air out and returned its wrinkled tired body to the stewardess, and immediately asked for an electric shaver, which KLM was obliged to give to tourist

64

class passengers on demand. The stewardess brought the shaver, which reminded me of a beach pebble highly polished by the sea, and the soldier in civilian clothes quickly found the outlet hidden in the arm of his seat, and, showing his technical skill, deftly plugged in the shaver. He shaved, and then, giving her a meaningful wink, he handed the shaver back to the stewardess, who not only lacked a sense of humour but all trace of sex-appeal as well.

As I looked at these American soldiers, decent fellows, I couldn't make myself believe that they could do much harm. Warm feelings were roused particularly by my neighbour, a straightforward, level-headed sort of fellow, obviously good at his work, with his stubby, but skilled fingers and his close cropped intelligent head.

The third soldier left no impression. He was sitting somewhere behind and somehow kept his dark, almost charred, face hidden between his two palms, which were pressed against his window.

I took another look at my shoes and again felt assured that they were no worse than the two hundred or two hundred and fifty perfectly polished shoes in the plane, first-class and tourist. So far so good. It calmed me somewhat, as though I had taken fifteen drops of valocordin.

But what's waiting for me over there, on the other side of the Atlantic? Where will I be able to clean my shoes?

I remembered that in large standard American

hotels they don't clean your shoes for you, and again I felt uneasy. I began to think about the continent I was slowly approaching and was seized by a presentiment of trouble, not great trouble, but bad enough —something humiliating connected with my shoes. Now I knew for certain that there was a man somewhere in New York who had been waiting a long time to do me some harm. He wants to take something very precious away from me. My life? I don't know. Maybe. I froze in advance, aware of my impotence and isolation, and I imagined myself coming face to face one fine day with this faceless man somewhere in the depths of a hypothetical New York street which possessed none of those objective details for which I, as both a writer and a man, had such a passion.

My God, what am I in for?

The pleasant landscape of old England receded imperceptibly into nowhere and gave way to the black, charred rocks of the Scottish coast. The sunless aluminium sky was reflected in a still sea. And immediately other islands appeared, just as rocky but known as Ireland. That was the last thing I saw of the world I was so rashly leaving for reasons I did not know.

It was the same morning dragging on, the morning which had begun, God knows when, on a fog-bound aerodrome, where like model figures we had stood on the hexagonal paving slabs of a runway. Several times

I had adjusted my watch, on each occasion losing time which for some unaccountable reason was lost forever.

It was only ten to ten on that same morning and our airliner was already hanging at a great height above an Atlantic shrouded by white mist, like a fly hovering above an aluminium saucepan set on the slow fire of a scorching sunny morning in which the hot foam of boiling milk was rising, though not enough to come to a head and run over.

Time—that strange entity which doesn't even get a reference of its own in philosophical dictionaries but has to run in harness with space—time seemed to stand still because we were moving in the same direction as the sun, east to west, and at commensurate speed, though the sun was slightly faster. Thus our progress through space could be determined by our lag behind the sun. We were trying to cross the boundary of today's morning, but the morning stretched monstrously in time and space, reluctant to cross over into noon, so that it seemed to me with my narrow local conception of time that I would never escape the captivity of this endless Atlantic day, and would never see the sun set. And in the land where I had left all those dear to me it was already night and above the sharp roofs the chiselled stars of the Great Bear were twinkling in the black sky.

I will never see the sun set, and I am passing into eternity without seeing a starry sky for the last time.

Yes that's the best: Rushing to the Stars.

67

The most depressing thing was the sense of a loss of time. Even my watch stopped keeping it with its accustomed mechanical accuracy. I could only determine the passage of time by the shine on my shoes, which gradually dimmed without apparent reason, just like everything else in the world. My shoes revealed a capacity to grow old. My wonderful young shoes grew up before my eyes, becoming duller than they had been in their youth. But of course they had a long way to go till evening and still further before night with its irreparable shabbiness, its scratches, its worn-down heels and greyish starlight.

I looked at them as at a watch, and I was horrified at the thought that, like my body, and my shoes, my so-called spirit was also ageing. It, too, was covered with the scratches of time, the greyish starlight tarnish of eternity whose infinite duration is determined by the law of the conservation of matter.

All the while the presentiment of the colossal unpleasantness which I was approaching continued to grow and intensify in me. Obviously this was the result of irritations which the outside world inflicted on my nervous system. Let's call them signals from the future.

Who can give me back my lost time?

Meanwhile the endless day over the Atlantic dragged on and on and on, and I don't know how it would all have ended if our plane had suddenly, by some miracle, brought its speed up to that of the sun. I would then have sunk into an endless day, without morning or evening, infinitely long, like the full text of the Bible, with all its repetitions and variants. Condemned to eternal wakefulness, I would have been turned to ash by the endless light and the infinite fatigue of everlasting life. Luckily our four-engined snail crawled along under the Atlantic clouds a little more slowly than the sun. It seemed to crawl with great effort and the blades of its airscrews did not merge but seemed to flash slowly round in the wrong direction with stubborn persistence.

In spite of all its efforts the snail could not crawl out of its little house, and so the sun gradually left us, and the endless tormenting day slowly turned into a tormenting evening which suddenly announced itself in the distance like a Sinai in the clouds from which the rays of Moses's light, smoky and purple, beamed upwards. A little further the clouds stretched like biblical lions above invisible Greenland, or maybe not Greenland but the Labrador peninsula. After this, the milky white lights gradually came on and the interior of the aeroplane seemed to close in on itself, renounced by the outside world where evening was driving out day and night was driving out evening. I shielded my eyes with my hands and lent against the gently vibrating window but saw nothing except the fireside glow of the engines and a few stars in the dark, dense sky.

I became aware of the hundred and fifty passengers behind me. They looked exhausted as they lay back in their reclining seats. Next to me dozed the American atom-soldier and I could feel the human warmth of his shoulder.

It is impossible to determine how much time has gone by if one has no conception of what time is. Half a dozen times we were served with food, mineral water, tea, coffee and fruit on little plastic trays. I dozed off half a dozen times only to wake up again each time.

Suddenly my neighbour lent across me and I felt the heat of his large body. He looked out of the window and said contentedly :

'Long Island.'

I saw the night through the window, it was like a seam of coal. Through its whole length right up to the horizon, moving slowly and silently in the opposite direction coloured signals were cut into it, a whole complicated system of signals : full stops, dotted lines, solid lines, geometrical figures, parabolas. They made me think of an inhabited continent with its own nocturnal life which I did not yet understand. I saw rows of white and bright green fluorescent lights along immeasurably long city highways, coloured traffic-lights, the gleaming bodies of moving cars, ellipses of illuminated stadiums with minute figures of running sportsmen, the suspension cables of bridges, the port-holes of transatlantic liners, and rotating lighthouses, their narrow beams scanning the horizon with the speed of a second-hand. Beneath me at fantastic depth floated nocturnal New York which in spite of its brilliance

70

could not turn night to day, so powerfully black was this night. And in the darkness of this unknown continent, in its mysterious depths, someone was lying in wait for me, poised to strike me down— me, a solitary traveller suddenly thrown over here from another world, not the old world, but perhaps one even newer than this.

Oh, if only you knew how lonely and defenceless I felt coming down the gangway as high as a two-storey house. I entered the purplish-green inferno of the near-tropical New York night—oppressive, humid—airless, and I walked along the uniformly lit corridors of the customs building, corridors that seemed cut into the frozen body of an iceberg. Lit from all sides I had no shadow. The air was conditioned and for a few minutes I enjoyed the artificial coolness. Then under the gaze of a beautiful customs girl, a smart blonde with the self-assured eyes of a filmstar and a pistol in her white holster, I took my slow-moving suitcase off the illuminated conveyor-belt and plunged again into the hot greenish-purple night, where no kind of artificial light could possibly dispel for me the black-ness of that infernal near-tropical August midnight on an unknown continent, where instead of Celsius the temperature was shown as Fahrenheit, which mon-strously exaggerated it, so that the damp heat seemed even more unbearable.

In my room on the twenty-third floor of a standard tourist hotel, where a colour reproduction of a winter landscape by Utrillo hung on the grey plaster wall over my interior-sprung bed, the heat of the night and the airlessness seemed even more terrible than outside. There was no air-conditioning. Instead there was a special cooling unit with a fan, set into the lower half of the square American window and hanging over the street, rather like a window-box. I immediately turned the plastic knob and a penetrating sepulchral stream of cold air blew into the darkened room, missing my hot sweaty face, and I had to turn another plastic knob in order to direct the cold stream onto the head of the bed. Now my face was blasted at an angle by a biting stream of icy air. One torture replaced another—the sub-tropical airlessness was replaced by an antarctic wind blowing with grim persistence diagonally from the window to the bed, in the dim night of that clean but depressing tourist-class room, from which I had a view of a cluster of half-lit skyscrapers and a spire, up and down which every sixty seconds ran a chain of electric lights, spelling out the minutes and hours of New York time.

I dropped off into a deathlike sleep and when I woke up I felt that the sepulchral wind from the cooler was still moving my hair, and through the window—the typical American window that opened like that

72

of a railroad car—over the familiar cluster of sky-scrapers, white Atlantic clouds were scudding in the fresh blue sky, and over the Hudson river which I could glimpse between buildings, sea-gulls were wheeling. I went downstairs and out on to the street. It was early Sunday morning and no one was about. Somewhere church bells were ringing, the sun was gilding the tip of the Columbus Column in Central Park, empty gin and vodka bottles lay about in the dry August grass, in which black granite rocks stuck out here and there; tawny little squirrels in shabby thread-bare coats came trustingly up to me, looking like little girls with nice bulging eyes. Sometimes a car in a hurry raced silently past, taking a happy couple out of town for their Sunday jaunt, he a plain young man, she a dazzling goddess, tall, slim, with streaming gold hair. I had no idea where I was and what I was doing. I was being led, as they used to say, by the mysterious force of destiny. In reality I was obeying the signals coming from my environment and I went from street to street, crossing narrow squares, straight into the trap set for me in one of the thoroughfares of that mostly brick-built, fairly old city. At every step I was con-fronted by scenes and images which I took to be distress signals. The seedy emptiness of these poor districts scared me. I was sure that at any moment, perhaps round that corner, I would be robbed. But what could they get from me of any value? A yellow certificate of vaccination and forty paper dollars with slightly scorched corners, securely pinned into my inside pocket. I wouldn't give them up even if someone stuck a silent automatic into my guts from that telephone booth.

No sign of a policeman or a passer-by, not a single witness. Everything was deserted, everything was locked up, people were either at prayer or relaxing. Everywhere weekend litter lay around, and even next to the brick fire-station, or the brick façade of the Franklin Delano Roosevelt Clinic there were no watchmen, no guards or doormen.

The signals became especially persistent in the narrow triangular Lincoln Square just at the moment when, among the dusty August foliage of the city trees, I caught sight of the sinister head of Dante in a medieval iron helmet. Amid all his circles of Hell he presaged nothing good, nor did the miniature, though fairly hefty, replica of the Statue of Liberty, a crude imitation stuck up on the roof of a five-storey house by some crank who was abusing his right as a free American citizen to do what he liked with his property. At first I even stepped back when I saw this familiar female figure above me with her raised torch. She was not made of greenish bronze but was quite black, as if moulded from pitch. But although it was supposed to be art, it was a hundred times uglier than the round water tanks erected on iron tripods on the roofs of other buildings—industrial silhouettes constantly looming in the distance before me.

I was standing there gaping when a long car nearly knocked me over. It was being energetically driven by

74

a young-looking old woman wearing a white silk suit so closely printed with black spots that it might almost have been a black suit with white spots. Next to the lady, looking through a curved windscreen which was topped with a soft sun-shade, sat a large pointer in a jewelled collar. It was also darkish white with black spots, or rather black with white spots, perfectly chosen to go with the black and white get-up of the young-looking, trim old woman, who flew past me on her way to bathe at Jones Beach—yet another signal foretelling imminent disaster.

Even more sinister was another car—no less long and luxurious—in whose spacious interior travelled a suit. Not a man in a suit, but just a suit by itself. Elegant, newly pressed, it was hanging on a thin wire hanger, hooked to the roof of the interior. It was quite ready to wear and go visiting in, even the corner of a clean linen handkerchief was peeping out of the breast pocket. Under my very nose the car with the suit stopped, the liveried chauffeur got out on to the side-walk, opened the car door with a slight bow and helped the suit out; lifting it high up he carried it carefully through the red door of a private house which was thrown open before him by a man wearing the morning coat of a head footman. After a few seconds the car moved off and I was again left alone, quite alone, that Sunday morning in Manhattan, feeling a certain humiliation because the suit had passed right under my nose without paying me the slightest attention and without even apologising for wafting Yardley's English

75

lavender in my face. At that instant I got it into my head that I was being watched from behind a brick corner by a kidney-shaped eye.

I was not going to run away from this inevitable meeting and boldly I turned the corner. But no one was there. I saw another street just as empty and as brick-built as the first. But there was something special in it: a small sickly tree, miraculously growing next to an old house with a black stone staircase which led straight from the street to separate front doors on the first floor.

Later I saw many such staircases in Harlem.

I still can't forget that scene: the black stone staircase with its shabby handrail, the sickly tree, the typical New York window without a frame, with the raisable lower sash, as in a railroad car, and at this window, hung with bird-cages and flowerpots, there was an exquisite young girl of about fourteen, pale in her sad beauty, with long hair falling in an old-fashioned style on her thin shoulders, thin half-bare arms and long fingers with which she was gracefully touching her childlike oval chin and soft neck, encircled by pale blue stone beads. She was half-woman, half-child and tenderly and sadly she was looking at a boy who was sitting on the doorstep as if at her feet, his red Irish head resting on his knees.

I realised that they were in love and also that they had nowhere to go outside New York on this stifling August Sunday. I understood that this was their paradise, their happiness, their grief, their hopelessness, their all. They shot a glance at my slightly dusty shoes and again sank back into their sorrowful, pitiful happiness in the shade of the only little tree in the whole street, with its fragile feathery leaves, its slightly unpleasant nutty smell, a tree which in the south we call the *chumak* tree.

I passed a row of a dozen or more garbage cans, their lids bulging with all kinds of rubbish : the leftovers of Saturday night, lobster shells, cardboard boxes, rotten grapefruit skins. I passed the big red doors of a fire station, then a dump piled with old car wrecks and thickly overgrown with weeds, which reminded me of my childhood and the Moldavanka. Then I passed a filling station where there was no one and the pistols of the filling pumps gleamed in the sun. Several times I had to step over dark streams, still wet, of children's urine running off the brick walls across the sidewalk.

And the bells exhausted me with their incessant ringing, reminding me of Sunday.

I lay like a corpse in the desert.

Again I turned a corner and found myself in a street which evidently ran parallel to the Hudson right from the Battery and up past charred wooden piers, which still smelled of burning for miles and miles. The street was all brick. One side of it was sharply lit

77

by the sun. The other was plunged in musty black shadow, with empty bars, clothing stores, dry cleaners, laundries, and Italian food stores, their windows hung with whole bunches of straw-covered bottles of *Ruffino* chianti looking like mandolins, and strings of Spanish onions, grey scabby plaits of garlic, and sticks of dry Milan salami wrapped in silver paper.

This was Tenth Avenue, empty from end to end, and looking as though it had been sawn down the middle by a sharp dividing line of light.

In fact, the avenue had only seemed at first to be empty, but this had been an optical illusion, for I at once noticed far ahead, at least a mile away down the avenue, a little man who came round a corner and stood still, looking at me. Although he was a long way off, I could plainly see his plump figure, shabby jacket, and the pasty face of an old failure, a derelict who would do anything for a pittance. What struck me was that he was looking at my feet, literally studying my shoes. I looked at them too, and was horrified. Till then I had thought they had a perfectly decent appearance. How dare I go out for a Sunday walk in such dust-covered shoes!

Behind the little man I noticed a shoe-cleaning booth. I had once seen just such a booth in Moscow near the public baths on the Neglinnaya. The little man was still looking at me with a hypnotic stare and he even made a slight half-gesture, as though he was trying to allay my vigilance and at the same time draw me into his trap.

I approached with the cautious steps of a sleep-walker. The booth was locked up with an ordinary, rather clumsy East European padlock from the early nineteenth century, and I was relieved. But the stranger quickly clicked it open with a key and flung wide the plywood door. Actually, there was nothing frightening about it. No black magic. What could be more straightforward? Your shoes get dusty, you go into a shoe-shine booth and come out in gleaming, incredibly black shoes which immediately, at one glance, put you back into the society of decent people, This is what is done by all civilised mankind. And still I hesitated. In addition to the round sum of forty dollars which I had safely tucked away in my breast pocket, I also had put away in a special little pocket a certain amount of change : seventy-four cents. From time to time I would slip my fingers into the little pocket and feel the coins deep down—the weighty silver half-dollar which seemed to me a small fortune, and twenty-four cents in various small coins for minor street expenses. But I didn't know how much it cost to have shoes cleaned. Actually I had heard it said that it could cost about fifteen or even twenty cents. There are no fixed rates. It's all a matter of free enterprise. They told me you could get your shoes cleaned perfectly well by a Negro in the subway for as little as ten cents, but of course they wouldn't have the same shine. If you wanted your shoes to shine like glass you had to pay for it. I was ready to pay up. But within certain limits. I was even prepared to hand over all my loose change for a shine. That would have been quite a lot. But never mind, after all I had a long Sunday ahead of me in New York. I couldn't very well spend it loafing about the streets and bars in dirty shoes, especially as I was going to visit two world famous museums, the Metropolitan and the Modern Art, and if there was still time the Solomon Guggenheim, which looks like the four-tier gun-turret of a super-dreadnought. How could I enter these shrines in such neglected shoes? It would be an outrage against world art.

One could not stand in shabby worn-out shoes before El Greco's 'Revelation of St John'. Or Renoir's 'Madame Charpentier', that black-browed lady in her purple-black dress with her purple-black eyes and hair. She seemed to be made of Parisian butter, and her two exquisite little daughters were so like her in their pale blue frocks. The St Bernard lay on the carpet, its purple-black silken fur with white spots matching the mistress herself. All of them together—madame, the girls, and the dog—were somehow the epitome of that rich, artistic, inaccessible Parisian life at the end of the century, to appear before which in unpolished shoes would be equivalent to sacrilege. To say nothing of the laughing, dismembered horse, and the devastating electric light which flares for the last time before universal atomic destruction in Picasso's 'Guernica' at the Museum of Modern Art. The stairs and floors, black as starlit night, lead you to an enormous window, giving onto an inner court, where you suddenly see, in the middle of an immaculate, bright-green lawn three old

Russian birch trees with drooping branches, as though painted by Nesterov, and silky-white virgin trunks, decorated with black strokes by the brushes of the best abstract painters—Malevich, or even Kandinsky himself.

How could I defile all this with my unpolished shoes?

The stranger was standing beside his booth trying to lure me into his den with different signs, and in different languages he tried to talk me into having my shoes cleaned.

'English?'

'No!'

'Italiano?'

'No!'

'Swedish?'

'No!'

That was as far as he could go.

'Français?' I asked hopefully.

'No!' he answered, and gently nudged me towards the plywood door of his booth.

'Deutsch?' I asked in desperation.

He spread his hands sorrowfully and asked:

'Hispano?'

'No.' I answered glumly.

He was middle-aged, flabby and short-winded, in a threadbare jacket and crumpled shirt, its collar loose, and the heavy brass stud, green with age, had rubbed a red mark on his neck. He had a bald head and bags under his eyes, like an old heart-sufferer, and he reeked of stale Italian cooking: onions fried in rancid

olive oil, and garlic. He was unshaven. A typical
Neapolitan *lazzarone* straight out of some hovel in
Santa Lucia. Except that he wasn't the excitable type.
On the contrary, he was slow-moving, because every
movement made him pant asthmatically with a wheez-
ing and gurgling sound.

'Russo?' I asked without hope.

'No,' he said panting.

We were both sweating.

He elbowed me towards the high chair and helped
me clamber up—it was like ascending a throne. My
shoes were then on a level with his grey unshaven chin,
a chin which would have done any Roman emperor
proud, and he threw my shoes a glance which was at
once contemptuous and yet greedy.

We had no common language. We had no other
means of communication. We were deaf mutes to each
other. We could only express ourselves by dint of
facial movements, like mimes. The old Italian seemed
to be a born mime.

'Well, *eccellenzo*, shall I clean your shoes for you?'
his disdainful face enquired.

'And how much will it cost?' I asked silently, with
the most varied body movements and gestures, even
writing a question mark in the air with my forefinger.

He understood.

'Twenty-five cents', he replied by means of facial
expressions, and just to be sure he mumbled it in
English.

I couldn't believe my ears; with a somewhat exaggerated expression of horror on my face I asked, with my eyebrows, cheeks and lips:

'What! Twenty-five cents? A quarter of a dollar just for a clean?'

'Yes', the bags under his eyes replied with inflexible sorrow.

'Why so much?' asked the wrinkles on my forehead. '*Warum? Pourquoi? Why?*'

Like Nero surveying Rome laid waste, he gazed majestically around at the old half-demolished houses of the district, where there would arise a grandiose, ultramodern Music Centre, and he answered me with a whole series of gestures, body movements, grimaces and signs which, without words, conveyed a complete picture of a New York Sunday in summer, with its faint ringing of churchbells, its emptiness, heat, lack of people and its laws against doing any business on a Sunday.

I understood: everything around was shut, there was nowhere else to get your shoes cleaned, he had opened up specially for me, risking unpleasantness with his union, therefore I had to pay double. I looked at my feet and finally decided that it was simply not proper to spend Sunday in New York wearing such shoes, and gave in.

I said in Russian, 'All right, okay, fine', and '*Bien. Good.*'

Then with an indescribably lazy manner he got a brush and in two symbolic rather than real movements, like those of a languid aristocrat, he flicked the dust from my shoes, which didn't look any the better for it. That done, he gave a sigh and wiped his grey-brown-crimson neck with his handkerchief. Then he poked around on the sort of shelves you get in similar establishments all over the world: here he kept various kinds of insoles, laces, soles and heels, screws, groovers, and other bits and pieces, and he held out a pair of laces wrapped in cellophane.

'Buy them!' said his face.

So, the old rogue wants to make money out of me, eh? Not on your life! I wasn't born yesterday!

'No!' my whole being cried out. '*No! Nein! Non!*'

He flung the packet carelessly back on the shelf and with eyes, which had suddenly become playful, like Brighello's, he nodded towards coloured portraits of naked and half-naked beauties which had been cut out of illustrated magazines, with a two-letter, five-digit, New York telephone number, scrawled with a joiner's pencil alongside each of them.

'What about this, then?' his old pimp's face enquired, but as I waved my arms in confusion, he poured a look of scorn over me and gave my shoes another flick. Then he got a bottle and took out the stopper, which had a piece of wadding wired to it, and he lightly wiped over the scuffed welts of my shoes, after which he gave them a final flick with a velvet and said with a gesture:

'Finished!'

What? Is that all? I couldn't believe my eyes. But there in front of me, lying firmly in the air, like an ashtray, was his grey palm with black life-lines, horny callouses, Mounts of Venus and all the other chiromantic details. And I warily laid out my change on that palm. Twenty-four cents. I said goodbye to them with tears in my eyes, as though they were my own children. That was all. I was short of one measly little cent, practically nothing.

But the old man was looking at me with unyielding insistence and he kept his palm firmly stuck out under my nose.

'Isn't that enough?' my whole being said, striving at the same instant somehow to reconcile Slav generosity with American hard-headedness.

But he felt so sure of himself as master of the situation that he didn't even reply.

'Twenty-five cents.' His whole being had turned to cast iron and it spoke with icy determination.

There was nothing to be done! Apparently he had the law on his side, or at any rate all the power of the trade unions. I gave in. Naturally I didn't feel like changing my nice heavy, pretty silver half-dollar. But what could I do? I was in his hands. So I collected all my bits of change from his rigid palm and replaced them with a beautiful silver fifty-cent piece. Without looking at it he threw it into his bulging coat pocket, turned his bent back on me and began to put away his pads and brushes.

'What about my change?' I exclaimed in Russian, aware that things had gone beyond my control.

He said nothing, but his back conveyed that there

wasn't going to be any change.

'Why? What right have you? *Warum? Pourquoi? Perché?* That is not honest. *Das ist nicht gut. C'est très mauvais. No buono.* After all we did agree to twenty-five cents!'

For the sake of greater clarity, I wrote a big twenty-five followed by an enormous question-mark in the air with a trembling forefinger, and added an exclamation mark twelve inches high.

'No!' he said sharply, shaking his head, and over each of my shoes he wrote the number 25 with a blue-black marble finger-nail. Then he inserted a plus sign between them, an equal sign after, and then clearly depicted the number 50.

I moaned as though I'd been shot when I realised that this louse had reckoned twenty-five not for both shoes but for each. I could do nothing with him: that was how he had interpreted our agreement. What could I do? What?

Punch him on the nose? But he had the law on his side, whereas I had no witnesses and I was only a lone and elderly foreigner with no contacts, no friends, cast into this distant land of dreams and groping my way around like a blind man.

I felt so sorry for myself that I was ready to lie down on the scorching pavement next to a rather weathered brick wall, under an iron fire-escape and cry out to the whole of Tenth Avenue that I'd been cheated, robbed, tricked, like the world's biggest sucker . . . But what could I do about it? Nothing! I couldn't even go and

86

complain to the UN General Assembly, whose smooth glass edifice rose up, like a Swedish bookcase, eabov the iron bridges and concrete supports of East River Drive. After all, I didn't have the status of even the most undeveloped country.

I was a mere private individual.

So I gave in, once again sinking down into the depths of secret dreams, which never reached up to my conscious mind, but lay deep on the dark unlit bottom of that substance which is still known as the soul.

And meanwhile he pushed me out of the booth with his massive body, gently, quite respectfully, I might almost say in a friendly way, and then he put back the padlock. From the depths of my slumber I looked at him, old and sick with a diseased bladder, and high blood pressure that made him pant, his trembling, swollen shiny hands, the red canvas sneakers on his bare feet, the old Italian straw hat with its coloured ribbon, like the snake in one of Conan Doyle's stories, and suddenly it wasn't myself I felt sorry for, but him. I imagined that he was the father or even the grandfather of that woman-child whom I had just seen in the window of the old brick house, with its façade disfigured by zigzagging iron fire-escapes and catwalks, among the bird-cages full of turquoise lovebirds, canaries, and chattering starlings. I felt like having a good, deep, sweet cry, and I forgave the old rogue and remembered my first love.

After that I spent a magnificent day, my first in New York.

Mitch came to fetch me with his girl. She was wearing a typically American bright summer frock, and he was wearing a dark summer suit, rough-textured and tight-waisted, which made his figure seem even more lanky. He took me round Manhattan in the deep-blue convertible Cadillac he had hired.

We all sat together in front, as on a school bench, pressed cosily together. The girl smelt strongly of 'Mitsuoko'. We drove like mad along roads elevated on white stilts, dived into white glazed tunnels under the Hudson, where for a few minutes we were swallowed up in the city night with its disturbing system of signal lights; we flew out into the sunlight, careered round dizzy bends, headed back, sped with the speed of sound across the new George Washington suspension bridge, compared with which the famous Brooklyn Bridge, of Mayakovsky fame, is as nothing; we flew —a fly through the middle of the suspended structure like a great harp with white strings. Mitch wanted to show me some wonderful highway which had sixteen lanes all going in one direction, but he couldn't find it and so we sped round and round Manhattan, crossing from one highway to another, and always on one side or the other, behind and in front of us, we saw the bright silhouettes of skyscrapers, the criss-cross of shining steel girders, beams, and scaffolding above burnt-out ruins of loading wharves. Sometimes we hit the yellow-opal smoke of a still-smouldering margarine factory, which spread over New York the baleful shadow of its eruption, like the classical eruption of Vesuvius.

88

catastrophe

The smooth but very steep bends kept throwing us together, and we sped on and on like mad things amid the white jazz of New York.

The town was particularly beautiful at the height of winter when snow eddied in the red-hot crannies of Times Square to the frantic din of Salvation Army pipes and drums, when it cascaded down from the metallic peaks of the sky-scrapers, turning car parks into deep graveyard snowdrifts, lit up by the moving reds of traffic lights and advertisements, and when, on a quiet mild morning, you could stand on the long steps of the New York Public Library between the two stone lions and see a third lion made out of snow by New York children and students. Those three lions gazed with their white eyes at the richest street in the world, Fifth Avenue, and at the famous Gothic churches, such as St. Patrick's Cathedral, or St. Thomas's Church, known as the 'Little Church round the Corner'. Next to them the latest skyscrapers look like corset boxes—tall, narrow, aluminium, glass cases, in which apparently these churches are locked up overnight, together with their porches, doors, marble belfries and even, it seems, their gargoyles, like those on the cornices of Notre Dame in Paris. This setting was completely natural for the somewhat fantastic appearance of one man, who suddenly arose beside me on the library steps, for all the world like a fourth lion with portentously raised eyebrows. I believe that he was one of a succession of reincarnations of the late lamented talking cat or even, worse still, of my

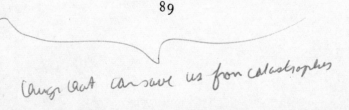
Cruys Cat can save us from catastrophes

long-lost miserable companion, the human wood-pecker, if you remember him, only he was thinner on top. At that moment I heard his hot breath and his voice, distorted by time and space, mumbling confidently in my ear: 'I must warn you. Be more careful. Don't admire everything so openly. What did you see in their George Washington Bridge? It's a load of crap. It's just like our Crimea Bridge, only a bit longer. Be extremely careful in what you say, or you might get framed without realising it.'

He sounded as though his grossly swollen tongue hardly fitted his mouth, so that ordinary words, though they did manage somehow to get out, came out some-what distorted, while long or technical words, like for instance 'neo-colonialism', crawled out of his half-formed fat little mouth into the light of day completely truncated, without vowels, nothing but consonants: nclnlsm, which did not however prevent him from being extremely eloquent.

'Let me tell you, I know what I'm talking about, I've been through the mill. Imagine the scene: they send me off to America, to the City of the Yellow Devil.'

I could indeed imagine it.

'I arrive, I buy some visiting cards in Woolworths, I dress like a man of the world, hire a car on credit, and so on. Thank God, I can't complain of lack of taste. One thing I have got is taste. You can see that yourself: I look just like a foreigner, right? Seventeen inch terylene trousers, without cuffs, narrow shoes, vents in the back of my jacket, nylon shirt, a sober tie with an abstract pattern, thin gilt chain. Everything okay. I get an invitation to dinner. I go. Here's the set-up: a business lunch in the Palm Court of the Waldorf Astoria. Cardinal Spellman, Rockefeller Junior, the Mayor of New York, Robert F. Wagner, our representative on world standards, Sidorov, ladies, gentlemen, representatives of influential circles in Wall Street. On my left sits the film-star, Agatha Brovman, 'Miss Hollywood of 1939'. The lunch is by candlelight of course. Crystal, silver, linen napkins, nothing imitation. Only the best! Naturally my nerves are strained but I give no sign of it and act the perfect gentleman. And then what do you think? The bastards trapped me with a provocation! The lunch comes to an end, waiters in white silk stockings bring round crystal finger-bowls. Now I'm an old hand, I'm not caught out so easily. I know what's what. I know the score. I've read the handbook: if they give you a bowl of water after lunch, whatever you do, don't drink it, it's not lemonade, it's for rinsing your fingers. Some of our fellows have fallen down badly on that one, but not me! I take the bowl and I begin to wash my hands in it for everyone there to see. But it turned out to be pineapple. Just think of it! In full view of the whole Waldorf Astoria I washed my hands in a pineapple dessert. Imagine, and it even turns slightly blue, sort of purple!'

'Well, of course, they sent for me and said: "You didn't go down too well in the City of the Yellow Devil,

91

Fedya, did you? We'll have to send you to a different continent. We'll fix up something for you there." So tomorrow I'm off. Mark my words: here they'll trap you before you know where you are. And God forbid that you should ever wash your hands in pineapple. Well, perhaps we'll meet again.'

He rummaged in his briefcase and handed me a small dog-eared visiting card, printed in Latin characters with the words 'Alfred Parasyuk, intellectual'.

It was the talking cat all over again!

The Americans made it plain to me, of course with great tact, that one really should not be over-enthusiastic about New York, because New York isn't America.

'Well, what is it, then?'

'Anything you like, but not America. If you want to see the real America you have to go and look for it in some other part of the continent.'

'Very well, I'll go and look.'

And I flew to Washington D.C., though it could hardly be called flying, that colourless aerial transit over the expanses of the eastern part of the North American continent in the long airtight cabin of a passenger plane. The cabin was lined with silver-patterned synthetic fabrics and it had secret cavities in the panels, which at night became like charts of the night sky, as I saw subsequently in the course of my several trips across the United States after nightfall.

The seat covers reeked of Virginia tobacco, and I saw two silent travellers at opposite ends of the empty first-class compartment. One was black, the other white.

It was the first time I had ever seen a Negro like that. He was faultlessly elegant, in a dark, lightweight suit, well mannered and evidently rich, with the fine sensitive features of a handsome European, a snow-white collar around a long, slightly feminine neck, and on one of his musical fingers glimmered a pale, very tasteful ring—it was very thin, like a new moon set in the shadows of his narrow velvety hand with its dusky-pink palm.

I had already seen eyes like that somewhere, eyes that looked straight into your soul as though through the slits of a mask.

'Excellent. Tomorrow I'll put you to sleep a better way. I promise you won't know a thing. And now sleep well.'

'Doctor,' I said, 'You have promised to put me to sleep, and that's fine, but can you promise to wake me up afterwards?'

He didn't appreciate my joke, he said nothing in reply and slipped out of the ward.

Perhaps my Negro companion was a doctor who had no time for the psychoanalytical approach of the 'great Freud' to functional psychic disorders. Perhaps he was conducting research, on behalf of some powerful pharmaceutical corporation, into purely medicinal methods for the cure and prevention of neurological and psychic disorders.

The white man was an ordinary American general, evidently a senior one. He was wearing a waterproof silk tunic the colour of onion-skin, with a crimson watered silk lining and a long, very reliable double zip. His straight army trousers were tucked into fairly high boots, his suede-gloved hands lay on his bony knees, and in the rack above his head was a large briefcase. He had a typical general's face : rigorously shaved, muscular, resolute, with handsome eyebrows, the face of a fifty- to sixty-year old man, who was not a hard drinker, but a steady one, a man prepared to perform any military action, even the most terrifying, if the circumstances demanded it, or on orders from above. If it were not for his large general's hat with its American eagle and small lacquered peak worn slightly cocked in the Cossack style (as in the old Tsarist army), he could be taken for Wrangel or Kolchak, or one of the other counter-revolutionary generals of the Intervention period. In his half-closed eyes under his bushy Irish eyebrows flickered tiny mirrored reflections of half-naked little men : bamboo huts blazed, bazookas fired, a stifling red fleece of burning napalm crawled over the ground and the jungle was drowned in poisonous fumes, and above it hung fat-bellied dragonfly helicopters with feebly upturned tails.

These two United States citizens, so different from

one another in appearance, were bound to each other by the unbreakable bonds of an ancient crime, for which neither was responsible ; they were united by all the might of the American state more securely than night to day, which exist simultaneously on this planet, chasing on each others' heels, white day and black night with all its senseless dreams and suppressed desires.

Meanwhile, an emigrant from a totally different world, having entered as it were a zone of spiritual weightlessness, I almost floated in my tipped-back seat somewhere on the edge of night and day. I had finished my grapefruit and the enormous toasted sandwiches of canned ham and processed cheese, which were decorated with damp lettuce leaves, and covered with ringlets of mayonnaise. Now I was holding a laughably weightless plastic cup, and the stewardess, who was wearing a sexy cap on her colour-less hair, poured into it a thick stream of heavy golden coffee, above which wreathed a divinely bitter vapour.

ascent back to consciousness

They prepared me in the morning; that is, they took out my old false teeth, removed my steel wristwatch, which was green with age, shaved my entire body, after which, without more ado, some young nurses briskly, with evident gusto, wheeled me on a trolley along a cold corridor, covered with squeaky Atlantic-coloured linoleum. Then they took me down in the

95

service lift and again even more quickly rolled me in a new direction along a similar deserted and sterile Atlantic corridor into the operating theatre, where the doors opened up before us by themselves, as in the New York International Airport, and I saw blue people, mainly exquisite young women wearing half-masks. They laid my body on the narrow, hard table under the round, still unlit arc light, and I finally resigned myself to whatever might come . . .

Meanwhile the expanses of wintry America, wooded, sometimes mountainous, a bit green, with decadent clouds on the horizon, continued to float past my window. When the scale of the terrain began to increase, I deduced that we were making a smooth descent. By some entirely incomprehensible visual association I correctly recognised towns which I had never seen before, towns which I was flying over for the first time in my life in the company of my two silent angels, one black as night, the other white as day.

New Jersey, Philadelphia, Baltimore—they were all behind us.

And then I saw, quite close up to us, a smoothly curving highway with broken white lines down the middle, and cars moving in both directions, not too many, not too fast, flat like cigarette cases. It skirted a tall, severe, electrical transformer, painted bright orange-red, so bright that it almost shone among the drab winter lawns and thin-leafed spruces, and I realised we were approaching Washington's new, ultramodern Dulles Airport. But this didn't cheer me up at all because I had the feeling that here in the capital of the United States it would be the same story as in New York.

'Washington isn't America.'

'What is it, then?'

'Whatever you like, but not America. It's a staging post where the transients are changed every four years. To find the real America you have to look elsewhere.'

'Where?'

'I don't know.'

'In the South?'

'Perhaps. It depends on your political views.'

'In the South-west?'

'If you leave your conscience behind.'

'In the West?'

'Maybe, I'm not sure.'

'But seriously?'

'Just keep looking.'

It was odd and depressing. Wherever I went in the United States I heard the same thing: this isn't the real America. You have come to the wrong place. Look for the real America anywhere else, but not here. Just keep looking.

Then I realised that there is not a single American who believes that he lives in the real America. He is sure that in some other state there is a real, genuine America, his promised land. It's hard for him to believe that the place where he lives is the great, one and only America that everybody knows.

I saw Washington, Houston, Los Angeles, San Francisco, Denver, Chicago, Boston, and finally the ominous city of New York with which my search for the real America had actually begun.

All this is not to mention my journey through the mountain passes of Nevada, a rugged plateau where white layers of snow alternated with the wine-red and yellowish layers of geological strata which are occasionally embroidered, as it were, with the green wool of conifers, so that it looked like a motif in Belorussian folk art. Our aluminium train passed one dizzying height topped by the icy organ of a frozen water-fall out of which it was no more possible to coax the slightest sound or the faintest groan than it was from my mute soul. Here too, over the frozen and snow-covered Colorado river, dotted with the tracks, large and small, of various wild animals, including perhaps reindeer, I was able to sit under the glass dome of the two-tiered tourist train and watch an infinitely long-drawn-out North American sunset.

But I realised the whole futility of my journey only when I at last glimpsed, through the window of the French plane flying me back across the Atlantic, the sand of Long Beach and Jones Beach, the snow covered forests of Canada, the Labrador peninsula and then the blue Atlantic Ocean flecked here and there with white waves, and the murky shadow of an atomic submarine carrying nuclear rockets.

I was returning with empty hands and had nowhere been able to find the true, the real America which, as I can now admit, I had not in actual fact been trying to find. For me America was the last hope of perhaps seeing once more the woman whom I had loved as a boy, or rather as a very young man since, when we met each other, she was fifteen or thereabouts while I was a little over sixteen. Or perhaps it was the other way round—she was sixteen and I was fifteen. But this no longer mattered. For all I knew, she had died long ago, leaving behind only a name which, because of some strange superstition, I am afraid not only to write down, but even to say out loud. Any human word recorded in writing or uttered by the voice is nothing more than a distorted reflection of the thing itself, an approximate likeness, a product of the workings of a secondary system of communications. Let her name remain lying in the depths of my consciousness, like a dream that was never dreamt.

Most likely she had completely forgotten me, not only because we had never been particularly close, but also because I was not altogether sure that she even realised that I had fallen in love with her for ever on that mauve March evening. A whole group of us had come home after a walk along the seashore with its summer cottages still shuttered ; we were looking in last year's dead leaves for small pale violets, the first violets of the spring with their faint delicate scent of cucumbers. Then she had gone to her friend's place to clean her shoes and comb her hair. I shall never forget how, standing in the hall in front of the mirror in its walnut frame, she had taken off her school hat, made of beaver and fitted with a bright green velvet band, and a round school badge. Her mouth was full of pins which she took out of her hair one after another. I suddenly saw the whole mass of her chestnut hair, tinged with red at the ends. It had flopped down on her straight childish back which was criss-crossed by the shoulder straps of her serge school pinafore. On her small feet she wore buttoned shoes and her dark green school dress came down to her ankles. Not at all pretty, she was small in height and had an undistinguished, slightly freckled face. Her cheeks were like a baby frog's, her chin was tiny, she had hazel eyes with puffy lids, feminine but without any individuality, which, as I understood later, was the very thing that was individual about her. As she held the pins in her mouth, her cheeks seemed even more like those of a baby frog. Her reddish eyebrows—those of a well brought up, diligent school-girl—were set in a frown. Her narrow sleeves were fringed with lace and out of them peeped the wrists of her small hands, still childishly red, with unevenly pared nails on which I noticed a few white spots—a sure sign that she would shortly be receiving some presents. These spots made her nails a little bluish, almost giving them the appearance of marble. Her flat chest under the black pinafore scarcely breathed. And I suddenly realised with horror that I had fallen in love with her for ever. Not for one second did I doubt the significance of what had happened, and I was horrified because already then I knew that from now on I should always love her, but that she would never love me. And I was overcome by a deep grief which I cannot describe because it had no cause and, like absolute silence, no outer expression.

We stood face to face in the vast world—she a school-girl and I, a school-boy in my black flannel school-jacket with its worn tarnished silver buttons. Round my neck under my vest I wore a small enamel cross together with a little canvas bag in which were sewn two heads of garlic. According to my aunt, these would protect me from scarlet fever and other disasters. Alas, they protected me neither from scarlet fever nor from the worse disaster of a life-time's unrequited love. But who knows, perhaps after all this eternal love is just a figment of my imagination?

Maurois says that one cannot live simultaneously in two worlds—the real world and the world of the imagination, and that anyone who tries to do so is doomed to failure. I am sure that Maurois is wrong: it is the person who tries to live in only one of them who is doomed to failure, since he is cheating himself, denying himself half of life's beauty and wisdom.

I have always lived in two dimensions. For me the one was inconceivable without the other and to separate them would have meant turning art either into an abstraction or into an insipid process of registration. Only the blending of the two elements can create an art which is truly beautiful. This perhaps is the essence of *mauvisme*.

Looking out of a large window which had formerly

given onto a flourishing garden full of the feather-like foliage of white acacias and the deep blue of a sunny southern noonday, I saw a girl hiding behind a bush in bloom, between two young black cypresses. She was fair haired, and stood daintily in a gay dress on a sand path which was pink from the heat. I fancied that she was secretly watching me. I lowered the hot canvas blind and went on with my writing. When I am writing, time disappears for me and does not stand in the way of my imagination . . .

If I were a liquid, say a small sluggish river, then I would not have to be lifted from the trolley on to the operating table but instead space could be slightly tilted and I could simply be poured from one level to another, so that my tormented body would reproduce the classical, broken posture in the deposition from the cross : head hanging down, legs dangling, and the sunken-ribbed body in the arms of disciples . . .

When at last I raised the blind, the yellow evening had almost come, but the girl was still there standing stock still in her place. I left the room, but when I returned in the morning and looked through the window I again saw the girl. It all seemed very strange to me, even sinister, but after a closer look I realised my mistake. There was no girl at all behind the bush, but only the bush itself, a pink bush in full flower between two young cypresses, which I had taken for a girl in a coloured dress. The bush seemed to be watching me from the far end of the sun-lit garden. But there was no girl at all, or if there was, it must have been Lyudmila in an invisible cap in a Magician's garden. Or rather there had been a girl there very much earlier, half a century ago perhaps, and then she really had stood on tiptoe, like a ballerina, on the pathway covered with sand and jagged sea shells, and she had watched me and perhaps somebody else as well. Where is the line between reality and imagination here? And what did it matter whether the thing was a pink bush or a seventeen-year-old girl? And suddenly I again looked out of the window and really did see a girl in a gaily coloured dress in the place where the bush was. This time there was no mistake because she had a watering-can in her hands from which sparkling jets of water sprouted like twisting horsetails. She smiled at me and went away with the watering-can, leaving an empty place between the two young cypresses. But I only had to turn away for a moment for the familiar pink bush to reappear in this empty space, while all trace of the girl had disappeared.

Something like this, or something very remotely resembling it, happened to me in Washington that day when I suddenly noticed a flitting movement quite near where I was standing. I turned round, but didn't see anything. I was standing in the corridor on the twelfth floor of the Statler Hilton Hotel waiting for the elevator : a glowing red arrow, short and thick, showed that the elevator was on a higher floor, but would soon be coming. I was standing there alone. From a hidden loudspeaker came the soft strains of a Brazilian Bossanova played on a trumpet—an agonising piece of music which was as interminably long-drawn-out as if some invisible person were writing a single word with a grey pencil in an unknown language, a word stretching over thousands of miles of monotonous space—on an infinitely long wall dividing the world into two equal halves along the equator. The elevator came down silently and stopped, the two halves of its thick bronze door opened noiselessly, and I stepped into its luxurious interior, feeling under the soles of my shoes the soft springy floor covered with a thick carpet of synthetic fur. And at that quite inscrutable moment when my body was no longer in the corridor, but was not yet standing in the elevator, something again made a flitting motion near by—at about the same level as my ears—and I had the impression that a dove had flown by. But the two halves of the bronze door closed silently and softly, almost without my feeling anything. Together with the elevator packed with ladies and gentlemen, I fell down an abyss and came out at ground level into the lobby where the floor was covered by a single nylon carpet measuring several hundred square yards. Passing the porter's desk, I noticed a table with a flat pile of letters which kept on growing all the time as long envelopes fell softly one on top of another from somewhere above. I still didn't see the connection between these letters and the flitting of dove's wings which I had noticed while waiting for the elevator in the corridor upstairs. That evening, however, as soon as I returned to my functionally designed room, and I stepped out of the elevator into the corridor, dead silent except for the Bossanova which was still playing its haunting tune, something white and dove-like again flitted near my face and vanished. I stopped and, with the wariness of a madman who suspects that somebody is secretly watching, I took a careful look round in the impenetrable nocturnal silence of this respectable hotel with the cracked Brazilian tune seeping through it. I examined every inch of the wall, the maid's table, on which there were cups and saucers, and suddenly at the height of my head I noticed a little glass window and under it a highly polished brass plate with the sort of slit that mail boxes have. At that very moment a letter flew past behind the glass—a long envelope with a blue sticker 'By Airmail' and an uncancelled stamp with the profile of George Washington in a white wig and a pigtail. This is how letters are mailed in large American hotels. They are thrown into this slit on any floor and they fall down, flitting past the little windows, until they land softly on the porter's desk to be picked up by the mail.

The white doves of letters had flown past me as though by way of a signal that the time had come for me too, taking advantage of the force of gravity, to mail a letter in this way.

'Stay at home and expect me between the 5th and 12th of this month, since I do not know exactly when I shall get to your town. Perhaps this is the last chance we shall have of seeing each other in this life. Do not miss it.'

I signed the letter with my name in full, but I addressed her by the affectionate form of her name which I had used as a child.

They were hauntingly sad, those winter days in Washington, lit by a gentle sun which was not yet that of spring, though it was no longer altogether a winter sun. It is generally like this in the first week after the Christmas holidays. The festive season had gone by, leaving in its wake wreaths of holly or mistletoe, which were decked with coloured ribbons, and hung over the shining red doors of grey frame houses with their white windows and the slender balustrades of their verandas. It had also left behind uncleared drifts of dirty snow which gave a rather backwoods appearance to the streets of Washington. In the Gothic windows of the brand new churches, which were lit up like theatre sets, the farewell candles of the festival that had now gone by still glowed on with a rose-coloured light. Christ had been born, grown to manhood and then gone up to heaven, crossing his long legs with the red holes where they had been pierced by nails. There were also empty cribs, bundles of straw, horned heads of oxen with dilated nostrils, the golden crowns of the Kings and the precious gifts of the Magi, plaster models of which I saw everywhere; on the vast lawns of university and medical centres, at the entrance to hotels, in the playgrounds of schools. They were electrified and had thick cables running to them. The blue star of Bethlehem had vanished from the frosty sky and a small winter moon of a bright sunflower colour stood infinitely high up in a marble sky over the right bank of the old Indian river Potomac, over the deers' antlers in the National Park, over the identical crosses of Arlington Cemetery, where President Kennedy was not yet buried, and over the brick buildings of a factory near an old-fashioned stone bridge with mighty bulls in the heavy style of English Victorian architecture. Under the bare trees lone figures of people walking appeared from time to time. Among them I saw a Red Indian gliding silently over the fallen green leaves in moccasins and holding a tomahawk decorated with a fringe. He had straight bluish black hair hanging down on both sides of a face which looked like baked clay. Then I saw Militia Major George Washington, tall and lanky in his red uniform and three-cornered hat, riding with a look of mad determination to visit a widow of his acquaintance. And as the ghosts of the Redskin and Washington crossed the ominous glades of Arlington Cemetery, President Kennedy slept peacefully in the White House.

In front of the hotel was the reinforced concrete wigwam of a nightclub and next to it a huge Indian totem pole with a black and red, monstrously painted mask.

The feeling of loneliness which had overcome me at the moment when I had parted my fingers and the long envelope with the hotel's beautiful round monogram had disappeared through the brass slit and, shifting its centre of gravity, sped downwards, was increasing all the time. I had sometimes had this feeling before, not often, but almost every time I had found myself abroad. A desperate, quite indescribable homesickness is something to which I am very prone. Now, mixed in with it, there was a feeling which I can only call a foreboding of death. Death was constantly in the air.

I felt its breath on the hair of my head, when in the middle of a wide screen I saw the blade of an open flick-knife reflecting the red and dark blue glimmer of a technicolour film. The cinema was filled with a horrified silence which was broken only by the hollow, reedy melody of that same Bossanova which throbbed rhythmically, like a dying heart. Shafts of light, first dark-blue, then pink and red and finally as white as in a mirror, passed slowly in turn, hurting the eyes, along the blade of the enormously magnified knife which was poised to enter someone's stomach and slit it open with an upward movement, so that the guts would spill out, while round about stood teenagers from the West Side, black and white, their hair curly or Irish red, splendid and hideous, motionless as statues—outcasts poor in spirit and repulsively beautiful in their youth.

In full sight of everybody the tender love of a helpless boy and girl was killed, desecrated and trampled underfoot while round about, instead of the triumphant crash of the silver and crystal jazz of the Rockefeller Center, there was now the black jazz of Harlem at night, the jazz of Small's Bar, the pitch-black and brick jazz of underground passage ways, of fire-proof walls, of steel nets and concrete back yards spattered with a mixture of oil and blood—slippery traps with no way out, where any moment you may trip against the red stub of a squat fire plug with a brass top reflecting the well of a brick yard, or some distant fire.

This desecrated love was dying in full view of everybody. There was no hope of help from any quarter, and a smartly dressed little Washington girl with mother-of-pearl nails, her flaxen hair done up in a pigtail, a plastic bag of popcorn in her trembling hand, was weeping. The whole of her delicate child's body was convulsed, and tears flowed from her dark-blue eyes down the sweet, rather spoilt, face of a schoolgirl, while a red-haired boy in jeans with two toy pistols in white lacquered holsters on his cowboy belt—he must have been her younger brother—said angrily to her :

'What are you crying for? It's nothing, they just had a fight with knives. And why did he have to get mixed up with that sister of his? Quit bawling, you're spoiling the show.'

But his voice broke, his mouth worked with uncontrollable anguish, the tears rolled down his freckled face, and his chin, which was that of a budding boxer, quivered childishly and at last he put his head on the shoulder of his elder sister and both of them, no longer ashamed of their tears, wept over the two young lovers from the West Side. This was a five o'clock matinée show in a cinema on the outskirts of Washington. The audience consisted mostly of school children—the girls had pony tails and the boys wore blue jeans and checked jackets. They were still on vacation, and sat there silently and horror-struck, watching the coloured screen which shone blackly in the darkness like oil cloth, and the tears flowed down their faces which were faintly lit up by the red darkroom lamps of the emergency exits.

From that moment I loved America.

Not the country of latter-day Caesars in democratic jackets and broad-brimmed Stetson hats, a country which seemed to me to be a modern version of the great Roman empire with all its brash sculptures and monuments, its stadiums, hippodromes and mausoleums, the marble seats of its law-givers, its curule aediles, the grandiose obelisks reflected in the long mirrors of rectangular lakes among the hills of the Indian forest and the English lawns of Washington. In the pale sky of the North American winter, the city lifts up, like a high, misty, Pope's tiara, its anti-artistic Capitol dome, thus somehow proclaiming over the whole of the western hemisphere the bitter truth once uttered by my friend Henri Barbusse that all domes, even the most magnificent, are simply ridiculous, like the things with which one used to snuff candles.

No. I fell in love with the America of those Washington school children—those boys and girls who, in the technicolour darkness of the matinée, wept over the broken and desecrated love of the white Romeo and the olive-skinned Juliet. Perhaps they were mourning their own defenceless youth.

I saw the tragedy of a great country which has chosen the path of Rome, not the path of Athens.

This is a retribution for the crime of their ancestors who reduced a whole people to slavery, deprived it of a motherland and left a terrible legacy to their descendants. The freed slaves are still slaves, because America has not become a home to them.

I saw that as long as black and white live side by side in America without merging or recognizing each other, and enjoying only formal equality as citizens of this immeasurably rich and cruel country, where tradition is stronger than law and where a white policeman may with impunity shoot a black boy, and a whole people have been deprived of their rights as free men—the United States will be the most unhappy country in the world, like a rich man stricken with cancer. There is no salvation or cure for him. In a Ku Klux Klan poster stuck on the wall of a house in Washington I read: 'We regard it as essential that the negro and all other coloured races in America should realise that they live in the land of the white race by favour of the whites. They should not forget that the white race is the ruling race by right of inheritance and that it does not intend to give up this right.' Apart from the moral vileness of these words they also contain an outright lie: the blacks do not live in the land of the white race by favour of the whites, but because the whites once brought them here by force, in chains, and turned them into beasts of burden, into slaves, so that to talk about 'favour' is simply to tell a bare-faced lie. And then 'the white race is the ruling class by right of inheritance' is also a lie. The white race lives in America by the right of the strong and cruel in the ancestral lands of coloured people, the Indians (called by the whites 'Redskins') whom they have almost completely wiped out and whose remnants they have confined for ever in special concentration camps, the so-called reservations. And as to the fact that the whites, the ruling race, do not intend to give up their right, what else can one expect from crude and enterprising conquerers who, using slave labour, have amassed untold wealth in the lands seized by them from others? So what is to be done? There are now 20 million blacks. But the chief question, which makes the blood of the present-day rulers of America run cold is: what will happen if there is a war? Can one rely on the stability of the American home front with these 20 million down-trodden and oppressed Negroes? In this I sensed the terrible tragedy of a black and white country which has grown out of a fearful crime for which one day or another, and quickly in the case of atomic war, there will come an even more fearful nemesis.

It was beginning to freeze slightly, a pink sunset gleamed on the roofs of the one-storey suburban houses, which looked like kiosks, on the barber shops, the automats, the drug stores, the neat service stations, and I walked down a street, broad in the provincial manner, on the outskirts of Washington, breathing the cold air in which were mingled, as it were, the most subtle hints of life and death in this time just before spring. But on the whole it was a bright, even cheerful, street in which practically everything was new : the laundries, the concrete lamp posts, the new red and green traffic lights at street crossings which, though not too garish, were very conspicuous and kept on flickering convulsively. For some reason it all looked rather like an exhibition.

But what I liked most of all here was a small house set back in an unfenced garden. It had a faultless lawn and two evergreen magnolias with layers of light snow on their dark glossy leaves. The tiny house was a delightful yellowish pink, like Turkish delight, with a Christmas wreath of mistletoe over the front door and two glass lamps shaped like torches which glowed wanly in the gathering dusk. The windows of the house were covered with white blinds which were lit from inside by a welcoming festive light. I immediately thought how nice and cosy it must be in this house where the friendly hosts were waiting for their guests— or perhaps the guests had already come and were now sitting at a mahogany Chippendale table before a Limoges dish of plum pudding which glowed with the blue flame of Jamaica rum?

My black thoughts were gone. Have you noticed how easily black thoughts are dispelled?

Over the door of the house there was a sign, an ornate affair written in white on a light-blue background, which I couldn't read, but the gist of which was undoubtedly a warm invitation to come inside. It was a house straight off a Christmas card. It seemed to offer a shining example of the happy way of life of an average American family, but at the same time there was something slightly cold and official about it, something specific to Washington, so that I even thought for a moment that it might be some kind of government office. But I immediately dismissed this strange thought and continued to look smilingly at the hospitably illuminated, though inscrutable windows.

'It would be nice to go into that little house and see what they're up to.'

'Do you like it?'

'Very much.'

'It's a funeral parlour of the All-American Service Company,' said my interpreter reading the sign. 'Shall we go in?'

I went through the entrance with its two electric torches and the wreath of holly, vividly picturing to myself how a small elderly lady in Los Angeles must have crossed the threshold of a house more or less like this and how she must have seen the showroom bathed in pinkish light where coffins of all shapes and sizes were beautifully exhibited by number, like suitcases. They were sturdy American models, the lids were broad, not high and tapering like ours, but flat and easy to manage so that they give no trouble during the burial. I had often seen coffins like this in American screen comedies, in plays, and then once on television.

A coffin just like this, covered by the Star Spangled Banner and strapped by army belts to an old gun carriage, stood before the steps of a cathedral where it was awaited by a Catholic bishop in his ominously divided mitre.

A year previously the husband of the woman to whom I sent the letter had died. I remembered him very vaguely as Kostya, a thin, polite student in a neat uniform and a dark-blue high collar above which showed the thin line of his starched shirt; I also remember very well the sham gold buttons embossed with eagles. And it is quite possible that a year ago she went into a parlour just like this one to choose a coffin and order some of the other necessary things such as funeral notices, visiting cards and a box of stationery with elegant envelopes and black borders round the paper. Perhaps she also bought a black veil and white funeral flowers, and also ordered a very much enlarged colour photograph, one of those remarkable imitation portraits in oil by a good realist painter who is able to produce a pretty good likeness of the original and at the same time give the face an important look, suitable for the occasion.

I still cannot understand why she married him of all people. And what happened to him in later life? He always seemed to me a mediocrity. In any case he was not worthy of her. Although, come to think of it, why shouldn't he have been worthy of her? He was a medical student from a good family with a little money of his own and a summer house on Sredni Fontan, which he had inherited. He had every prospect of becoming a general practitioner. He wasn't bad looking, some even thought him handsome. Altogether he was a perfectly respectable young man, a good match and probably madly in love with her. (That's how they used to talk in those days : 'he was madly in love with her'.) He must have gone to the front, not as a simple private, a volunteer or even as a lieutenant, but as a military doctor. His chances of being killed had thus been much lowered. And what was she, if one didn't count her mysterious charm which drove men out of their minds? (That was another thing they used to say in those days : 'she drives all the men out of their minds'.) If one is to put it without any verbal frills, she was simply a poor girl, the daughter of a bankrupt Bessarabian land-owner who had not provided for her, and she could scarcely have hoped, as people said then, for a better match. So it was all very natural. But I remember how terribly surprised I was by the news that she had got married, even though I had long ceased to love her by that time. But this surprise was nothing in comparison with what I felt late one evening in an unlit town when I blundered into their room and saw the large marriage bed covered with a red satin quilt (obviously part of her trousseau) and her eyelids flushed with excitement.

They stood in front of me happily embarrassed— this was their honeymoon and I was the first visitor who had come to see them in their small, rather poor room which they had found through an advertisement. They had not wished to live with either his or her parents, but had immediately declared their independence, particularly as the revolution was already on and all the old standards were crumbling. They were happy in their nest and her tiny fur slippers peeped out shyly from under the bed. I was struck most of all by the look of happiness on her now completely feminine face.

I stood in the door fidgeting with my officer's khaki cap—it had a hole where I had ripped off the badge, just as I had pulled off my epaulettes and chevrons. I had not seen her for a long time and this was my first visit to this room with its thick walls. She asked me to sit down and he—also in army tunic with a university badge, without epaulettes but in long student trousers with foot-straps—began to fuss with the kerosene primus in order to make some carrot tea, sweetened with fruit drops, which in those days was regarded as something of a luxury. He even began to wipe the glasses with a tea cloth, and I did not know where to look from acute embarrassment. I cursed myself for having been a wet rag as usual and agreeing to go and try to borrow money from them. 'She will certainly give you some,' my two friends had said. 'That's for sure—she's bound to have money, newly-weds always have money, and there's no other place to get any. And the main thing is that it's quite near by, so that we'll still have time to go in by the back entrance and get that Greek to sell us a few bottles of dry Armenian wine, the only wine still left in town. There is nothing worse than not having enough to drink. She loves you, she'll let you have some.' And they said that if I wouldn't go, then I was no friend and comrade but the lowest of traitors, a prig, and so forth. I said that I didn't want to make a fool of myself, and I could feel my lips quivering. But they shouted in chorus : 'Make a fool of yourself, make a fool of yourself! What does it matter if you make a fool of yourself?'

There was a noise in my head. I was full of drunken bravado and I boldly went up to her room while they waited for me in a doorway—both of them later became famous and you can find their names in any encyclopedia.

Of course, she immediately realised that I was drunk but she did not take fright and became even more friendly. A warm light came into her eyes.

'It's ages since I've seen you,' she said and called me by my pet name, as she had when we were children. 'Well, this is how we live. Sit down and tell me all about yourself.'

'I have come on business,' I said with an effort, calling her by her pet name. 'Lend me fifty roubles and I'll give it back to you not later than the day after tomorrow. On my word of honour I will.'

The relations between us had always been of a rather high-minded kind, on the level of what was then called 'platonic love', and it was by no means easy for me to get out these words. I would not have said them at all if I had not been drunk already. I almost broke the lacquered peak of my cap. She was even more embarrassed then I, but she didn't bat an eyelid.

'Oh, of course, of course.'

She whispered something to her husband who went up to the icon in front of which there were two half-burnt wedding candles and some wax orange blossom. From behind it he took a weird looking banknote for 50 roubles issued by Hetman Skoropadsky, money which was at that time circulating in the South. The note had a stylised, very starkly drawn picture by the famous illustrator Yegor Narbut, of a Ukrainian man and woman in national dress. It had a strange coat-of-arms shaped like a fig leaf, and I can still see the crude printing, the thick paper and bad colours—yellow and blue. It was already worth practically nothing.

'You needn't worry, I will definitely return it in a day or two. I'll bring it back myself. When is the best time to find you home?' I said, looking at her and marvelling at how good-looking, almost beautiful, she had become, and trying not to notice the new satin quilt, which seemed to reflect a crimson glow throughout the room, although at that time there was in fact no electricity—the current had been cut off, and the room was lit by an improvised oil-lamp. That was the last time we saw each other and the picture that remained in my mind was of him and her, the fifty roubles, the satin quilt, a dark courtyard, and my two friends with collars turned up waiting for me, huddled against the wall in a dark doorway, and then the deserted night street, slippery flagstones of volcanic rock, a wet granite sidewalk, the crack of a rifle behind a corner and the clatter of an armoured car which made the window panes tremble in the houses. This was the beginning of the uprising.

Kotovsky's cavalry, with red ribbons in the manes of their horses, swept over the steel-blue granite roadways, striking sparks with their horseshoes.

It may seem strange that, simultaneously with this, I saw standing on the window sill, placed one on top of the other, several round nickel containers with double handles made of wire. But we really do not know what time is. Perhaps it doesn't exist at all. At any rate everybody knows that 'there is no excellent beauty that hath not some strangeness in the proportion'. I didn't invent that, it was said by Francis Bacon, the father of English materialism.

The measure of strangeness consisted in the fact that a room filled with blue girls in gauze masks was reflected fairly realistically, even though slightly distorted and blurred, in the surface of the round containers. It was in some ways reminiscent of *Princess Turandot* with its captivating waltz played on combs. And just as I at last saw the winding sheet over my own prostrate body, the very bright, yet not too blinding light of the operating lamp hit me in the eyes from above, and behind me I felt the presence of the blazing six-winged seraphim before whom everything yielded.

With fingers as light as sleep he touched my eyes

and I saw from a height of twenty-six storeys the town of Houston, a disturbing mixture of old wooden houses with verandas running round them, and waste lots with white super-modern skyscrapers dotted around at random like rectangular plasticine towers, transistor sets and accordions. In the gaps between them one glimpsed the endless expanses of the Texan prairies and a sky streaked by the dull-pink and grey-blue rays of a Mexican sunset which looked as though it had been printed by lithograph at the beginning of the century on the glossy cover of a cowboy novel for reading on railroad journeys ('The famous cowboy Buffalo Bill, whirling his lassoo above his head, stands in the stirrups of his rearing mustang').

I looked down at the wide open spaces of Texas, trying to get my bearings by the setting sun and figuring out where the Gulf of Mexico, and Dallas, the chief city of the state should be.

A strange idea, or rather feeling, came over me as soon as I had moved into one of the glass cells of the Sheraton Hotel. From a distance it looked like a honeycomb placed on end among others of its kind, and in each of its cells there lived a man like a bee, or perhaps like a larva. I felt that my body and the hotel were a single entity. I was at once both a human being and part of the building. We shared the same general structure, and consisted of the same cells—we had the same metabolism, enzymes, chemical reactions, reflexes of the higher nervous system, functioning of the digestive tract, circulation and temperature which, in the shape of innumerable elevators, would rise silently to forty degrees, drop below zero or remain suspended for a moment in a state of anabiosis in the lobby. This enormous space was covered with shaggy yellow synthetic carpet and furnished with heavy morocco leather armchairs and bright red settees. Here one saw the usual habitués of hotel lobbies : interpreters, heads of delegations, company representatives, travelling salesmen, plainclothes men, detectives and journalists festooned with portable equipment—cameras of various kinds and old-fashioned flash bulbs. Here, in an oblong marble pool, out of which stuck a single graceful reed, a drake with a golden green rhomb of a side feather floated over the mosaic bottom in shallow blue water, and the scarcely perceptible circular movement of this artificial bird affected the pit of my stomach like a slight queasiness, like a reminder of latent heart disease. It was here that I made the discovery that man has the magical ability to turn for a moment into the object he is looking at. Suppose the whole of human life is nothing more than a series of such transformations?

During one trip out of Houston to a ranch I turned into one object after another. To begin with, I turned for a time into a motorway stretched over the Texan plain, which is hard and firm like the Novorossiisk steppe, with dry dusty flowers of the sort which are never free of traces of tar. Cut in two down the middle by vivid white dotted lines, I sped in opposite directions to the horizon with its apparitions of the latest kind of cracking plant and the mysterious silver globes of pumping stations. Below me—two or three, one on top of the other—there flashed by intertwining reinforced concrete structures over which asphalted replicas of me shot out in various directions, carrying traffic both ways and hurtling my body with irresistible force to various parts of Texas at a speed of eighty miles an hour— which meant that they were practically marking time. Then, for a short while, I was the sad winter sun of Texas, and also one of the first automobiles of the second half of the 19th century, the charming creation of a still rather immature technical genius—'the horseless carriage'. It had brightly polished brass lamps and a horn with a rubber bulb. This convoluted device barely managed to squeeze out of itself high-pitched sounds, like the cry of geese, which made horses shy away.

It was in just such a red automobile that Emile Zola drove to the Dreyfus trial, and it was like the carriage driven by that terrifying Mephistophelian chauffeur in the enormous goggles who is depicted in a brilliantly smudged manner in the Toulouse Lautrec lithograph.

Reverently preserved for posterity, spick and span and washed clean, with small morocco leather seats rearing above the comically small radiator, I had been converted by the force of my imagination into an automobile. I stood on a low round pedestal, surrounded by ferns and mosses, in the middle of a department store in the super-functional style of the second half of the twentieth century. It had been flung up in the midst of the empty, still uninhabited prairie at an intersection of some new State and Federal highways with their numerous exits, route signs and reinforced concrete lamp-posts, divinely curved like the stalks of artificial plants in the future when mankind will have learnt to create all the species of the organic world, giving them any shape he wishes. But what was the point, one may ask, of putting up this department store, a marvel of engineering and architectural skill, the acme of simplicity and comfort? Free of modernistic decorations or gimmicks, it was an inordinately huge, flat structure with glowing ceilings, lawns and flower beds set in the black and white marble of its vast floors, and was capable of storing within itself and showing off to best advantage millions of items ranging from the essential to the totally useless. Round about, the desert stretched as far as the eye could see to the cloudless horizon, and the few customers who drove out here from Houston from curiosity rather than necessity, merged into the background of the flat expanses of floor under the hidden lighting of the softly glowing ceilings. However it would be wrong to think that there was only desert round about. It was not entirely desert. It had been deftly and inconspicuously divided into building lots to which there already stretched a sophisticated underground network of plumbing, gas, telephone and electric cables, sewage and central heating—that whole complex system of circuits which was turning the earth into living flesh.

For a time I was flesh of the flesh of the dry Texan

earth, distinguishable from it only by virtue of my even more complicated circuit.

There was no difficulty at all about building a house on lots like these. Architecture was of no consequence. One could live comfortably in a simple wooden box which was instantly equipped with hot and cold water in the bathroom, heat in the hearth, a water closet, a shower, a television with ten channels of programmes relayed from New York, San Diego and Melbourne, a telephone of remarkable quality, fluorescent and concealed lighting, and ice in the refrigerator, so that one could immediately set up home here with one's beloved wife and begin to increase and multiply without further ado—if, of course, you had enough dollars to pay the first instalments for the land and all the rest. Incidentally, here, in the state of Texas, the problem of dollars was solved very simply. You didn't have to go into the bank for them. You could get your dollars outside, on the street : your car drives past a row of marble cabins set at an angle to each other. You stop at one of them and hand your cheque straight out of the car through a window with an automatic bronze grille, a bell rings, the grille clicks, a pretty girl-teller with a pistol under the counter hands you a wad of green notes, a lamp flashes, a camera hidden in the marble wall takes your picture, the bronze grille comes down and off you go about your business. The only thing not clear about this is : where do you get the cheque? They tell me that Marx has some interesting things to say on this point in *Das Kapital*. But better not talk about Marx in Texas—supposedly the richest oil state in America,—where I heard the epic tale of a certain lady, poor and getting on in life, who one fine day struck high octane oil on her small lot of land.

The Legend of the poor Widow: '... and then,' says the legend, 'the poor widow went to the bank where they immediately gave her a credit account of one million dollars so that she could buy everything she wanted.'

I don't know what she wanted, but I imagine that she was quickly and without difficulty able to satisfy all her current needs, and then invest the rest of her capital on advantageous terms in some underdeveloped or colonial country with cheap labour, after which she was received in the best society of the state. For a long time I was haunted by the image of this elderly Houston lady, and I think I must even have met her somewhere or other: in that department store in the middle of the prairie, as she was buying something she still didn't have, or at a dinner party by candle light (the ladies in evening dress and the men in black tie) at which for half an hour on end she stood talking to me in broken French with a strong Mexican accent about the comparative psychoanalysis of Tolstoy and Dostoevsky characters, while I (in well polished shoes and black silk tie) stood with a tall glass of gin and tonic wrapped in a paper napkin in which, ringing slightly, broken ice cubes floated like lilies. I also talked away in French, painfully digging out of my memory, now impaired by sclerosis, remnants of

French idioms which were like the fossilised vertebrae of pre-historic animals.

On her nose she had a hearing aid in the shape of a luxurious pair of spectacles studded with small diamonds and connected by a golden cord to a transistor battery. The latter was hidden somewhere in her breast under a precious stole of dark sand-coloured mink which shone with a priceless sheen by the light of the twisted wax candles placed here and there throughout the old-fashioned sitting room where the party was taking place.

She kept shifting her legs, which were as muscular as a race-horse's. Her silk-covered pointed shoes with very high heels and diamond buckles pawed the carpet, as though she were about to do the Madison, and her eyes, as sharp as a jackdaw's, looked straight into mine with the relentless condescension of a deaf school-ma'am. Without drawing breath she conversed in French, and out of her open mouth, equipped with the best brand of new false teeth and pink plastic gums from the most expensive and famous firm of dental fixtures, there issued a constant stream of brittle French phrases eked out when necessary by bastard German and even Italian words, all of which immediately produced in me a responding flow of eloquence.

It was like a minor version of the Tower of Babel, and this feeling was heightened by the sight of her hat which was constructed out of pink angel feathers and had a veil which partly concealed her passionate Savonarola face.

Next she passed to the problems of contemporary music, and she made an interesting observation: '. . . your famous composer (I can't pronounce his name), about whom I have read quite a lot in the New York papers, carried out a brilliant experiment and turned the popular tune "I'm going to Maxim's" from Lehar's *Merry Widow* into the theme of a symphony, and then, a few years later brilliantly turned Schubert's *Ave Maria* inside out to make an original number for a popular Soviet film . . .'

Seeing that I was about to lose consciousness, the old lady stopped for a moment and threw me a life-belt in the shape of the question: what did I think of the abstract artists? She was ecstatic when I said in reply that they are irrelevant to art, and to painting in particular, but that they are engaged rather in an unconscious effort to create a third system of communication. And then she was as thrilled as a child and even clapped her hands when I told her that I was the founder of a completely new literary school called *mauvisme* (from the French word for 'bad') the main point of which is that, since everybody writes so well nowadays, one must write badly, as badly as possible, and only then will one attract attention. Of course it's not so easy to learn to write badly because there is such a devil of a lot of competition, but it's well worth the effort and if you can really learn to write lousily, worse than anybody else, then world fame is guaranteed.

'Just think, I had never heard of it before!' she exclaimed despairingly. 'Texas is such a terrible backwoods for things like that! We are always the last to get to know about anything! But you really write worse than anybody else?'

'Almost. There is only one other person in the whole world who can write worse than me and that's my friend, the great Anatoli Gladilin, *mauviste* number 1.'

'That's a real eye-opener. Merci. Prosit,' she said, raising her ice-filled glass. Thereupon, in fulfilment of her duty as a hostess, she put me in her sports car and rushed me with the speed of death to the Sheraton Lincoln Hotel, where I was awaited by the familiar wooden duck relentlessly sailing its shallow pool.

After pushing various buttons I found myself in my functional room face to face with the Texan night sky which, tinted here and there with the glow of neon and argon, lay in long horizontal streaks in the cracks between the plastic slats of a blind fully drawn over the solitary, wall-length window of my room.

All alone now, I continued for a further brief period of my life to be that Houston lady, and I just couldn't rid my mind of those original thoughts concerning *mauvisme*, until I entered another incarnation as my hotel room, with all its aura of suspense, its gadgets, its two-way communication system, its innumerable Turkish towels and hygenically sterilised bath robes in stylish black. They were generously draped round the room or stacked in fluffy piles in the bathroom, which had a frosted green sliding glass partition dividing the bath from the shower where, by pressing various knobs, you could programme for yourself a shower of any temperature accurate to within $1\frac{1}{2}$ degrees one way or the other—degrees *Fahrenheit* of course!

At the head of my mechanically adjustable bed there was a remote control panel so that, without getting up, I could programme the environment of life in my room. By simply pressing a button I could control the room's temperature and humidity. I could learn the weather forecast, the atmospheric pressure, the latest from the stock exchange, the schedule for sports meetings and races, the latest news up to the minute, and last but not least, I could have myself woken up at any specified time—even though time as such doesn't really exist. I was simultaneously man and dwelling, so much was there in common between us, beginning with the regulated temperature of our bodies and ending with the pre-arranged hour of awakening. The room woke up first and then the occupant—if he wasn't already awake because of insomnia.

In the evenings I would press the button which determined the moment of my awakening the next morning. It would come more or less at the appointed time, but not all at once, as though wishing to break me in gently to the waking state without an excessively brusque interruption of my sleep. My sleep was full of passionate anticipation of my forthcoming meeting, and of disturbing dreams which it was impossible to

130

reconstruct later : nobody yet understands the physical mechanism of memory.

The room began to wake up first, gradually restoring the external, purely functional links, extremely important for the control process, between system and environment. To begin with, a small light came on all by itself in the tiny lobby. After that, something clicked softly in the control panel and began to murmur grumpily, like the body's blood beginning to pump with difficulty. I would open my eyes and jump up : who had switched on the light? The previous evening I had myself firmly closed the door of the room with the patent lock, as witness the tiny emerald lamp, a magic eye mounted in the outside door handle. Who had dared? But at this moment a second, stronger light lit up in the bathroom. Then the bed lamp above my head came on, bright, radiant and gold like a six-winged seraphim with a gauze mask on its face. Finally the whole suite was lit by a glow from the ceiling. The indicators on the control panel showed everything I had asked for the previous evening. The noise in the panel grew ominously and finally it emitted the shrill chimes of an electric bell, which I was not able to stop even after pressing all the buttons one after another. This interminable earsplitting clangour was driving me out of my mind, and water of the temperature I had asked for now began to rush down into the cobalt-blue bath, filling the room with the frantic hiss of a hot geyser. In despair I banged my fists on the control panel, but the apparatus would not stop and it continued with relentless persistence to carry out the programme I had fed into it. So I poured a jar of boiling water into it, and it stopped.

All this was strange enough, but even more terrible was the television set, this instrument which bears perhaps the greatest resemblance to the human brain, at least in its ability to convert signals coming from outside into living imprints of the surrounding world, into glowing, kinetic images of it. A large flat television set stood at the far end of the room at an angle to my bed, but I was able to switch it on any time I liked without getting up. All I had to do was find the right button in order to start something rather like a game of tag: all ten television programmes would quickly flash, one after another, across the super-sensitive, pleasantly convex screen of milky blue, chasing each other's tails and not giving me time to concentrate on any one of them. In order to catch and keep the programme I wanted, I had to press the button quickly at the right moment. But that seemed terribly difficult: I switched off a sequence about breaking in bucking broncos—fiendishly wild animals which threw their unfortunate riders by digging their front hooves into the ground and kicking up their hindlegs almost vertically. The cowboys bit the prairie dust and then lay still for ever on their backs, arms outstretched among the flowers. Suddenly the screen would begin to jump violently, deathly black streaks would shoot over it along glowing broken lines, and a new programme burst on the scene: two spacemen with thin antlers of antennae on their synthetic helmets sat side by side in a spaceship. They were working complicated and intricate controls, occasionally glancing through the black porthole in which one could see a huge, vivid white moon floating by. But at this point a secret door suddenly opened behind the two men, and in came the villain holding a pair of automatic atomic pistols, complete with silencers. One more second and shots would have flashed out, but just at that moment, interrupting the oppressive nightmare at this thrilling juncture, a large cake of toilet soap rolled out, or rather slid into close-up, shed its wrapping to reveal the deeply imprinted trademark of the firm, while the velvety bass voice of an ideally clean man—a husky mate and lover—ingratiatingly recommended one to wash oneself with this sweet-scented soap which was so elegant, inexpensive and kind to the skin. I pressed the buttons again, but the television set now got quite out of control. Sequences followed each other at horrifying speed, black streaks of death alternated with the white kaleidoscope of life, conjuring up people, landscapes, conventions, the baton of the Philadelphia Symphony Orchestra, stage shows, church services, aerodromes, rockets, and a white ice-hockey puck surrounded by swirling human shapes.

And then there was the performance of a world famous Russian eccentric with the pudgy figure of a jack-in-the-box and a stupidly hypocritical smile on his gap-toothed, ill-tempered mouth. He was showing off his favourite trick—the art of placing his hard-crowned felt hat on his bald head as though it was an inverted chamber pot, supported only by his ears. He had done this four times and was just about to take his bow, when suddenly a leg came out, kicked him in the backside, and sent him flying from the scene . . .

I could no longer understand anything, and was powerless to deal with this apparatus, which was quite out of control. It even seemed to me at times that the gadget had a completely independent existence and obeyed only its own whims. But the worst thing was that I could no longer give it orders, let alone stop it, make it silent and dead, bringing to an end the flickering light and the random snatches of music or human speech. It looked as though we had changed roles—I was no longer its master, but it was giving me orders through the control panel. It was forcibly hampering my thoughts, chasing them back and forth, and unconnected images, imposed on me by an alien will, flashed through my jaded brain.

I was no longer a free personality, but a controlled one. And what an ordeal that is, particularly if the instrument of control is a machine! I had become an appendage to this accursed, transistorised apparatus.

I was not free even in my dreams. An alien will, an external force drove them back and forth as it wished. And I mean literally 'back', although time is supposed to be irreversible, with every material process developing in one direction only—from past to future. But here in Houston, I discovered that at moments of extreme nervous tension or during a lengthy period of unconsciousness, there may be exceptions to this rule, so that time begins to run backwards, from the future to the past, bringing with it snatches of events that are still to happen. I do not know how to explain this phenomenon, but it happened to me here when, with a tremendous effort of the will, I at last broke free of the gadget's control and captured on the television screen several episodes from the future. Subsequently, about a year and a half later, in another place and at another time, I saw these same scenes again, but in their legitimate sequence, that is, in transit from the past to the future. But then, in Houston, they were interlopers from the future.

I saw the assassination of the President a year before it happened. I saw that street in the ill-fated town of Dallas, a street called Houston Street. I saw it jumping in all directions, because the cameraman taking shots of the President was riding in a car. Then another street began to jump—this time because the cameraman's hand was trembling. The President slipped from his seat and his head plunged downwards into the darkness, on to the knees of Jacqueline. Somebody jumped up and people began to run. A whole crowd of them moved rapidly in the same direction. All this happened about two hundred miles from Houston where for the first time in my life I witnessed the backward motion of time. Men in broad Texan hats, with the brims turned up, besieged the doors of the hospital to which the President had been taken. Then the crowd froze and parted to let through a priest who came out slowly between the two ranks, holding a prayer book to his breast. He was neatly dressed in a well fitting business suit and black silk tie and was wearing a black, broad-brimmed hat of the type worn both in Texas and the Vatican. His face was dispassionate and his eyes gazed straight ahead at a point a little higher up than is usual with ordinary people. He was already an extraordinary person. He was a priest who had suddenly become famous throughout the world.

Then, almost immediately, some policeman lead a handcuffed psychopath along a drab grey corridor. But before he could pass out of sight off the screen, a fat man nobody had noticed appeared from behind a wall and jabbed a pistol into the belly of the psychopath who slumped into the arms of the policeman and, in full view of the world, turned into a shadow; everybody then surrounded the fat man with the pistol, about to turn him too into a grey shadow, but at this moment the reel ended and when the screen flashed on again, I saw Jacqueline in a beige coat with a black fur collar running at the side of an ambulance, clutching at the steel door handles and vainly trying to open the rear door behind which lay the body of the President. Her face, shown in close up, was beautiful and tense, she had wide-set dark eyes and a short, slightly turned-up nose. Her head filled the screen for a while, and then quickly, like a school girl, she gathered up her coat and jumped onto the seat next to the driver. She was wearing a very short skirt, as was the style just then, and it revealed the well-formed legs of a young, rich and happy American woman who still did not quite realise that she was now a widow . . .

Then suddenly the whole screen was filled by a close-up of the 'human woodpecker' with the musical comedy name of Prokhindeikin.

Looking through the dark window of a plane of the Delta line, I had seen all I wanted of the night towns scattered like clusters of Christmas tree decorations over the wide spaces of the American continent, and now I stood in the room of a Los Angeles Hotel, next to a standard lamp, with a telephone pressed to my ear, and heard her voice. The most remarkable thing was that it was so unmistakably her voice, and nobody else's, and that she uttered my name with great feeling, and told me that she had been waiting for me a whole week, never leaving the house.

'Are you glad?' I asked.

'Enormously,' she replied, with the special, secret meaning with which she had always spoken this word in the old days. It was 'her' word. She sported it like a brooch with a semi-precious stone, and it marked her out among all the other girls she knew. It drove her admirers out of their minds. It was her trick—this way of pronouncing the word 'enormously' in a tone which one could invest with the most suggestive meaning.

'Do you like Brahms?'

'Enormously,' she would reply quietly, in a meaningful way that hinted at the depth, passion and richness of her inner being.

'Do you like the autumn?'

'Enormously,' and she half closed her hazel eyes behind lids which were bulbous and feminine.

'Do you like the spring?' The eyelids rose joyfully:

'Enormously!' and her eyes went straight through one, to the depths of one's soul.

Once, fighting the shyness for which I despised myself, I asked her in desperation, with a forced smile on my frozen lips: 'Do you like me?'

'Enormously,' came the earnest reply in a deep muted voice, and she looked straight at me with her not very pretty eyes, though they seemed beautiful to me.

Goodness how I suffered!

Sasha Miklashevsky, a rich and handsome student, once asked her: 'Do you like to go sailing by moonlight? I have a little boat at Langeron.' He was tall and well-built. She lifted her head, crowned with a bun of chestnut hair and looked up at him. He licked his small red lips as she said: 'Enormously.'

Later on we played at 'postman's knock'. When it was their turn they went into the next room and came out after a while with coy smiles that nearly drove me mad with jealousy. There I was a high-school boy whose girl was being stolen from him for everybody to see!

But all this was nothing in comparison with my

138

despair, even horror when many years later, after a long absence, after the war, after poison gas, battle wounds, the February Revolution and many affairs with various women, thinking that I had grown out of my youthful love, which seemed to me quite frivolous and even comic, I came to her and found in the drawing room a young man—a mere boy—a curly headed music student. Without taking his blazing, tender, imploring eyes off her, he was accompanying himself on an old piano, striking the yellow keys with the iron fingers of a virtuoso so passionately that all the plush covered furniture shook in this stuffy bourgeois drawing room and one could not hear the rattle of the empty drays racing past under the balcony down the Kherson hill to the Moldavanka. He was singing a popular song with the refrain 'I madly await your embraces' while she stood there, her mouth sensually half-open, her eyes half-closed as she watched his swiftly moving, thin, almost childlike hands with a ring of hair on one of his fingers ... His name was Raphael—I have forgotten his surname.

'Do you like him?' she asked me.

'Do you?'

'Enormously.'

At this moment I could have killed myself, if I had not, fortunately, left my officer's revolver at home.

At dawn both he and I walked home together through the deserted town which looked shabby after the meetings that had taken place there that day. He hurriedly walked alongside with a rather bouncing step over the dry rustling leaves of white acacia. Friendly and well disposed, he kept looking at my St George Cross which gleamed in the sea-green early morning light.

Now, forty years later in Los Angeles, the telephone pressed to my ear, my free hand resting on a small elegant edition of the Bible in English (printed in small type on very thin paper—an inevitable feature of any American hotel room), it seemed that I was not just talking with an old friend who was giving me instructions on how to find her house, but that I was taking some strange kind of oath. Through the window I could see the inner courtyard with square lawns, palm trees and magnolias, the corner of a light-grey concrete and glass multi-storey building, and in the distance two equally light-grey concrete structures over which roads passed at an angle to each other. On them was a sparse line of stationary automobiles which seemed to offer vivid proof that immobility is really only a form of movement. And finally there were the rows of high, reinforced concrete lamp-posts alternating with the even higher Washington palms, their disproportionately small tops like reddish brooms broken by the dry winter wind from Mexico, a cold merciless wind as harsh as emery paper which drives the long flat Pacific waves along the California beaches. These waves are just as wild and hostile to everything living as the angry seagulls which glide above them on outstretched wings, crying like cats in a murderously mechanical way.

The monotonously blue sky was polished by that same Mexican wind blowing from San Diego or somewhere over the dull orange plantations with their darkish-yellow artificial-looking fruits—one exactly like another—which were warmed from below by small kerosene lamps; it blew over evergreen poinsettia bushes spangled with bright red flowers clearly visible from afar like traffic lights; it blew over Disney-land, this incarnation of my childhood view of the world with its rubber elephants squirting water, as though from a hose, at a toy paddle-steamer, with its journeys by submarine in whose portholes silent pictures of a green underwater kingdom moved before me through streams of bubbles. And among the waving seaweed and murky fragments of shipwrecks were hidden all the treasures of my imagination: a hugh conch the ribbed halves of which, as though breathing, slowly opened up to reveal the unearthly rainbow whiteness of a pearl the size of a coconut; near a broken piece of mainmast, grown over with tropical moluscs, there was a green-bronze chest from which gold coins—real old pieces of eight—had spilled out onto the muddy sea bottom, and a sea monster looked at me with huge staring eyes while the Mexican wind still blew on— over the villa of Stravinsky whose name was itself just like a wintry blast from the depths of Mexico with all the wind, string, percussion and pizzicato instruments joined together in a counterpoint of genius; over a dogs' cemetery at the top of a bare hill; over the restaurants and studios of Hollywood; over the 'slanting cheek-bones' of the Pacific ocean beyond whose sultry horizon I thought I could vaguely make out, on the slopes of another hemisphere, the contours of my home country; over the evening street, where I at last found her dark house.

Even before I got there, I could make out her motionless figure, although in the dusk it merged almost completely with the bare, iron-black bush growing in front of her small single-storied house. One could have thought that she had been waiting for me here from time immemorial and had turned into a small grey statue. This idea did not strike me as odd, since the formal measurement of time artificially divorced from space, and its accepted division into years, hours, minutes and centuries, give only an arbitrary, distorted idea of true time. Breathing with difficulty I quickly walked up some stone steps to the top of a grass-grown slope—a fairly usual feature of any provincial American street—and stopped with my hat in my hand, scarcely able to believe that it was really she standing in front of me, and still thinking that one gets a much better idea of time, not from the sand trickling imperceptibly from one half of an hour-glass to the other, but from a simple stone turning 'in the course of time' into sand, or gradually turning back from sand into stone, and then again 'in the course of time', becoming sand. In this process one not only feels but actually sees the destructive or creative action of time undivorced from matter. To put it in another way, I can get a sense of time not from the mere passage of hours but by looking, for example, at my hand, already covered with the large brown spots of old age, and thus actually seeing the relentless deterioration of my body. When I held out my hand to her, I thought 'It's a quarter to eternity'. She must have read my thoughts, because she said: 'It's forty years.' Then she led me into her house. Here we were again, as once at the beginning of our lives, standing opposite each other, quite unique and unlike anybody else in the whole world, in the middle of a traditional, dimly lit American-style hall. It had an empty brick fireplace heated by a fierce gas flame which kept collapsing and then reconstituting itself again—the artificial, eery and excessively white flame of the rich Californian winter, colourlessly dazzling to the eyes and hot to the face, which one saw in practically all the local hallways and restaurants. Standing on a low oblong table for papers and magazines, hectically lit up by this deathly light, was an oil portrait, copied from a photograph and framed in silver, of a handsome man with a kind, but not very memorable face. Of course I would not have recognised 'Kostya' in this nearly full length portrait of a respectable looking gentleman. If the end of the moiré sash of an order had peeped out from under his waistcoat, one could easily have taken him for the president of some small European republic such as Portugal. All the paraphernalia surrounding him only heightened the impression: a massive writing set on which rested one fine hand wearing a slender wedding ring, and mahogany shelves with solidly bound books as background to the noble grey head of a good citizen.

She was about to say something—perhaps that it really was him, but she changed her mind and said nothing. Thus he was a witness, as it were, rather than a participant in our reunion which went on the whole of that night and for a few hours until my departure the next day, by which time we had drunk all the supplies of tea in the house. Little yellow tabs, marked Lipton, hung down in vast numbers from the lid of the English teapot in which there were cold soggy bags of thin paper filled with fine black Indian tea. These bags always astonished me by the remarkable way in which the paper soaked through without disintegrating, even in boiling water. We drank tea steadily till at last the little bags of Lipton left no room for any more water in the teapot and we had nothing to quench our thirst. This needless, contrived meeting seemed to me like a painful immersion in the depths of an infinitely deep sea dividing us with the heavy water of silence through which our words were exchanged with difficulty. They were somewhere on the verge of the consciousness, like undreamt dreams that leave no residue in the memory. The circuit through which we communicated was faulty and was constantly broken by disturbances coming from without—it was like a black and white blurring.

My real reason for coming here had been to find out whether she had once loved me. All my life I had been troubled by the question as to what had really happened,

but all our lives both she and I had been in a strange
kind of torpor, close to non-being. Like someone under
an anaesthetic who at the same time is aware that he is
asleep and desperately tries to wake up but, despite the
most intense mental effort, is not able to escape the
tenacious clutches of sleep, I could not tear through
the shroud of silence in which I was tightly wrapped.
I was already on the point of suffocation, prepared to
remain lying for ever under the fearful weight of the
miles of still water pressing down on me, when
suddenly, with a last effort of the will, I forced myself
to see a large window beyond which a sunny Russian
June morning shone very beautifully, though in a kind
of remote way. Everything was there in precise detail
—the tree-tops in the hospital garden, an angelic sky
in which, somewhere in the neighbourhood of
Kuntsevo, flowed the gentle purring whine of a jet
plane going in to land. And there too was the express-
way on which I had driven back and forth a hundred
times in my life, always entranced by the sight of a new
world in birth and by the multi-towered pyramidal
building which at night looked like a Christmas tree
with electric lamps. Amid the fields, meadows, and
woods there was a hint of chemical factories, rocket-
launching sites and the catapults of high-voltage power
lines traversing in every direction the unique, thrice-
blessed country of my soul which had given me so
many delights, so much inspiration, so many disappoint-
ments, so much happiness, so many sublime thoughts,
so many great and small achievements, so much love

and hatred (and sometimes despair), poetry, music, crude intoxication and divinely subtle dreams which came to me so sweetly and softly at dawn to the timid singing of the first nightingale—in a word, so much of everything that has made me what I am, or rather what I was, since I could no longer struggle free of the shroud of sleep. But suddenly, with a final effort which convulsed my whole being, I nevertheless managed to make myself ask, not in the words that really mattered, but in other words which startled me by their poverty :

'Tell me, why didn't you marry me?'

'I was young and silly,' she immediately replied with a kind of unthinking, wistful lightheartedness, as though she had been expecting this question. She had her head slightly on one side and was looking up at me a little, without wiping her eyes and with a resigned smile, and at that moment I saw on the wall behind her a vaguely familiar water-colour—the only thing which she had taken out of the country with her more than forty years ago. It was a Russian girl, almost a child, in a coloured kerchief. She was carrying an Easter candle held in a paper bag so that the March wind should not blow it out. The candle lit up her face in such a way that the lower part of her cheeks, which were as round and red as ripe apples, was bathed in a bright and gentle light, while the top half was in shadow, and her happy eyes with tinsel lights in each pupil looked at me innocently and brightly. I immediately remembered Blok's lines about the little boys and girls bringing home Easter candles and palms, and passers-by crossing themselves.

'Do you remember?' I asked and without a moment's hesitation, as though she had been reading my thoughts all the time, she recited the rest of the poem in a mechanical voice. Then she fell silent, but it was now my turn to read her thoughts and I could see what she saw: our first, last and only kiss, which had never really counted, because it was only the kiss that people exchange at Easter in the customary way.

It had happened next to the festive table laden with *kulich*, pink shavings of hyacinths, painted eggs round a green mound of watercress, a leg of ham and a silvery bottle of Shustov Bros. raspberry liqueur. She had stood there the morning after Easter, still a little sleepy, but with a freshly washed face, and she had looked at me expectantly, her arms slightly raised in their long lace sleeves which half-covered her fingers down to the polished nails. She looked at me with open curiosity: what was I going to do? This was the first time I had seen her out of her school uniform. Her light blouse was a little too big for her and through the tiny holes of the embroidery one could see pink silk straps, which didn't suit her at all, giving her girlish figure something of the appearance of a grown woman's.

'Christ is risen,' I said with rather more vigour than was required by the circumstances and diffidently stepped up to her. I was clean, well washed, and also suffering from lack of sleep. I smelled of my aunt's eau de cologne, my bristling hair was greasy with brilliantine and my new boots creaked.

'In truth He is risen,' she responded and asked with a smile: 'Should we kiss?'

'We must,' I said, controlling my breaking voice with some difficulty.

She put her hands on my shoulders and they smelt in an old-fashioned way of flowering elderberry—perhaps it was because the lace of her sleeves had gone a little yellow from age—and we duly kissed each other. I got a very close view of her cool, tightly closed lips spread in a smile, her small black birthmark, and her eyes which expressed nothing at all, not even embarrassment. It was also then that I saw her father for the first time, though I had often been in their house. But her father was never at home: he had always either just left or had not yet returned from his club.

He entered in a new frock coat and white waistcoat, and he was filling his wallet with stiff white cards intended for the visits he was about to make. She introduced me and we exchanged Easter greetings. He looked at me searchingly with a sort of curiosity I didn't understand, and then he shook my clammy hand and poured out some raspberry liqueur into two green glasses, one for him and one for me. We clinked glasses, drained them and I, who had never before touched any alcohol, immediately felt drunk from the vapours which filled my mouth, nose and throat with a delicious, burning raspberry taste, while outside, beyond the windows with their dry cracked putty, the enervating chimes of Easter bells in the Mikhailov monastery rang out. White clouds floated across a watery blue sky above lilac bushes with swollen buds and sparrows; the sun blazed on the mercury ball of an outdoor Réaumur thermometer; a fly came to life and crawled along the painted window sill. I looked with glazed eyes at her father, at his hard snow-white cuffs with gold cufflinks, at his firm close-cropped head resting easily on the short stocky body of a retired officer squandering away his wife's Moldavian estate at the card tables of the Nobleman's Assembly and in the Catherine Yacht Club.

'Do you remember my father?' she asked, continuing to read my thoughts in some incomprehensible way.

'I remember everything,' I replied sadly.

'So do I,' she said and we both fell silent. The silence lasted an incredibly long time. Then at last she decided to tell me what had evidently been on her mind for many years.

She put her hand, which was already the dry weightless hand of an old woman, on my shoulder and, with her eyes looking slightly upwards as usual, she said in the tone of a sister:

'You know, not long before his death my father opened a secret compartment in his writing desk and showed me, without saying anything, a photograph of your mother, the one where she is shown at the age of seventeen in a Sunday-school dress and a starched collar round her neck. You remember her dark oval face and Japanese-looking eyes? It seems they knew each other, your mother and my father. And I think'— she sighed deeply, almost inaudibly, 'that my father was once in love with your mother, perhaps he loved her till his dying day. You see the kind of thing that happened in our lives, my dear,' she added sadly.

By now we were standing again in front of the house, this time to say goodbye forever. I don't remember much of what she said to me that last time in our lives, as she gazed fixedly into my face.

'I wouldn't have recognised you on the street, but I would have in a train . . . When I heard that they'd shot you I went home and sat on the sofa, feeling quite numb. I couldn't even cry. I'd gone quite numb. I couldn't bend my fingers. I felt I'd turned to stone . . . I felt I was in a void . . . What a joy that it wasn't true and that you're alive, you're alive . . .'

'But suppose it is true, and I've been dead all this time?'

'That would mean we've both been dead.'

'Perhaps we have.'

And he tore out my sinful tongue.

A winter wind from Mexico was blowing over the roofs of Los Angeles. The dry Washington palms were rustling. I could see the slate strip of the Pacific and somewhere beyond the glowing distant horizon I could sense another continent where the land of my heart lay shimmering.

She was still standing on the threshold, small, dark

and motionless, and she was looking in horror at my charred wings. And when the enormous car was already gliding past the concrete lamp-posts and houses, I turned for the last time, for the very last time, and I saw her utterly motionless form which seemed to confirm once more that immobility is no more than a variant of movement. I saw her dark shape at the top of the slope, next to the bare, iron-like bush.

Later I again saw that plant, sprinkled with the bright red glowing flowers that herald the Californian winter, but I had forgotten its name. Its name was on the tip of my tongue, I strained my memory to the utmost, but I couldn't recall it—the associations had been obliterated and there was nobody to ask.

Now I'd lost practically all interest in America. It seemed to have lost its soul, a beautiful artificial country, like Disneyland. Why had I been so eager to come here?

Eternal love. Alfred Parasyuk. A book for a few readers. Poinsettia. Pale blue people. Only now in more detail.

'In Paris Kostya and I went every day at five to the Coupole but we never found you. Where were you hiding?'

What could I tell her? I was hiding at Barbusse's. I was in love with his *'Clarté'*. I used to gaze endlessly at his dark, narrow face, and at his hair, falling over his wide brow, as he leant towards me, and I listened to his voice in which, in those days, there rang for me the greatest truth of our time :

'Nobody realises what use could be got out of the treasures that are now being squandered, or what heights could be achieved by man's reborn mind, now confused, repressed, stifled by shameful slavery, by the accursed and infectious necessity of war, and by privileges which degrade human dignity. Nobody realises what the human mind might create in the future or what may hold sway over it. When the people achieve supreme power, literature and art—a new symphonic form of which is barely in embryo—will acquire unprecedented greatness, like everything else, in fact. National-minded coteries only cultivate narrowness and ignorance and are the death of originality. As for the national academies, whose authority rests on surviving superstitions, they are no more than a fancy picture frame for ruins. The domes of institutes which look so majestic from near-to, are really ridiculous, like those things once used for snuffing out candles. Everything must be relentlessly broadened and internationalised without limit. We must throw down the barriers, the people must be able to see the full light of day, they must see beautiful vistas. Patiently and heroically the path from man to man must be cleared ; at the moment it is strewn with corpses, and graven images obstruct the arc of the distant horizon from view. Everything should be remade according to the laws of simplicity. There is only one people, and one people only !'

And where was she? I thought to myself.

'I have nobody left any more. Nobody in the world. I can live well enough, but I am quite alone.'

That was the last thing I heard her say. And those pitiful words followed me day and night, first in the canyons of Nevada, where perhaps at that moment they were carrying out underground nuclear tests which I sensed through the stronger beating of my heart and the shock to my entire neuro-vascular system. Then they followed me among the steel girders of Chicago, in the morning winter twilight of its gangster slums, in the coal-black chinks between ancient skyscrapers and the latest sixty-storey towers of two inexpensive apartment houses, which stood alongside the incredibly long shoreline. They were shrouded in the clouds of frozen mist which constantly advance on the city from Lake Michigan, whose presence one could only vaguely sense by one's frozen eyelashes, by the leaden gleam, by the strong north wind, which stung the face with the burning cold of the unseen lake. Its waters had been turned to stone by the Canadian frost and the icy wastes of the Arctic. Finally, those pitiful words pursued me among the respectable brick houses and churches which give Boston its special, almost religious austerity and its air of tedium. In a silent multi-storey hospital, surrounded day and night by news photographers, reporters and TV cameramen, ninety-year old Robert Frost, the famous American poet, lay dying on a high bed in a private ward. Propped up by large fresh pillows, he was surrounded by flowers and gold-topped bottles of French champagne in ice-buckets, and he was holding forth without pause. He kept rolling his red eyes, which were awesome like a prophet's, and naive like a child's. They were set in the parchment of his rigid, blotched face, a face already covered by the brown finger-marks of eternity.

When I had last seen him, he had looked like an enormous boulder pressed into the earth by the great weight of centuries. He had seemed hunchbacked, his long arms had reached almost to the ground, his legs were short and stocky. Wearing a loose new suit and supported on the arms of admirers and Washington bureaucrats, he had walked among the columns and sculptures of Congress to bring his congratulations to the newly elected young and debonair President Kennedy. He had seemed to personify the America of Mark Twain and Longfellow—the old America shaking hands with the new.

Now he was lying in a high surgical bed with a glass in his hand, trying not to spill the Veuve Cliquot onto his snow-white gown, which exposed his parchment neck, mottled with the brown marks of old age. He stared at me and spoke in his high-flown prophetic Boston style, addressing somebody only he could see.

Perhaps he could see the charred wings behind my back and this made him even more agitated.

'It seems absurd to me when people say it won't take place. Believe me, it certainly can sometime. But if it does break out . . . I call on you to mark my words . . . Mankind, listen to what I have to say . . . In the name of a higher truth, if universal lunacy sets in, don't poison the wells, leave the apples on the trees in peace, so that the people can still their hunger and quench their thirst, if you don't want human life on earth to end altogether. That's all I have to say. And now you talk,' he said angrily as he made an effort to clink his glass with mine. He stared at me with his stubborn eyes, which at that moment suddenly seemed to me artificial, peering as it were, through the slits of a mottled mask, silently demanding my reply.

What could I say to him during that last minute of our earthly meeting? I could only do one thing—loudly proclaim the name of that Californian evergreen which is covered with bright red flowers in mid-winter, but I had forgotten the word, the one word that could save the world and us all. Feeling downcast, I remained silent but I could already hear within myself the distant voice of another great American poet born more than a century earlier in Boston :

And I said—'What is written, sweet Sister,
On the door of this legended tomb?'
She replied—'malume—malume—
'Tis the vault of thy lost malume!'

The French plane turned towards the ocean and I saw in the day's newspapers from Paris enormous funereal blocks of frozen slums and the corpses of people who had been killed by the cold the night before in Belleville. I saw pictures of firemen pumping water out of cellars where pipes had burst, and I learned that Beaujolais would be going up ten centimes the litre again. I dozed in expectation of Europe and all the time I felt pleasantly exhausted, like a man who has dived into a fearful abyss to salvage the marble statue of a goddess, and who now floats on the surface, half-dead from inhuman strain. But on his outstretched palms, amid the seaweed and pale blue sand running through his fingers, he holds nothing more than a figurine of a widow, who has been lying there on the bottom for several thousand years.

Yes, I remembered the waves of the Obera,
And the misty land of Nodd.

Perhaps it was all an experiment to set up yet another system of human communication?

Now, when I was returning from the land of Stravinsky to the land where they have turned Schubert inside out, gradually, second by second, the time that had vanished without explanation was returning to me, and, breath by breath, the life that had been sunk in hypnotic sleep returned also.

Yes, I remembered the shores of the Obera,
And the reed-shrouded ghosts of Nodd.

And the movement of monsters in the sea and the growth of the vine in the valley . . .

My wife, grey with worry, was still standing on the

hexagonal slabs of the runway, in which the signal lights of the airport were reflected, though they could scarcely pierce the night mist. Silently she took my arm, and as though nothing had happened, we set off along the forgotten street, where an old man in charred fingerless knitted gloves was roasting chestnuts, and above the brazier swirled thick clouds of frosty air, illuminated by the haze of blue light from the electric signs outside the *Théâtre de Sarah Bernhardt*, where the Emperor of the French was running around the stage in short boots, one hand stuck in his piqué waistcoat. We bought a bag of big roast chestnuts which burnt our fingers; but the charred husks came off easily and we ate the chestnuts like school children who have spent their last two sous on sweets and have got lost in the big city. I dropped a glove somewhere. My fingers froze and I blew on them to warm them up.

We wanted desperately to go back, back to where our little granddaughter was sleeping in her cradle, her hands clutching with all their might at the tiny starfish which we had picked up at low tide. We wanted to go back where, under the thick straw roof of the Norman barn, and under the majestic canopy, the Kozloviches were sleeping and dreaming of two Germanies, one Democratic and the other Federal, as though they couldn't decide which one to visit by tourist bus; where, in the little orchard under the flowering chestnut, the young milkmaid's scooter was lying on the ground, where she, her blonde hair mingled with the cropped hair of our son, Jackal, slept the blessed sleep of the righteous, a plump pink cheek resting on his bare arm, while on the floor were strewn a red dress, seamless nylon stockings and on the back of a chair hung a black bra with white buttons, and on the writing desk stood a milkcan and a pair of sneakers. Jackal himself was breathing heavily, and without his glasses he looked like a new-born kitten. We wanted to go back to where our daughter, Hyena, was fast asleep, her legs outstretched. Hidden under her pillow was a new novel by one of the best known modern *mauvistes*, and her husband, standing at his drawing-board with its heavy counterweight, was trying to work out how to make a model of the new system of communication. We wanted to return to the lawn where there was a half-burnt-out car in which those great travellers, the Ostapenkos, were happily asleep, and where huge automobiles made to the highest world standards slid silently along highways, reflecting in their paintwork the neon lights of hotels, and the urgent signals of filling stations, street signs, flashing advertisements, towns and theatres. It was there we had loved one another so tenderly and so sadly.

But apparently at that instant something happened, because now we could recognise nothing around us. Actually there was nothing there to recognise. There was only the charred corner of an electric transformer, sectioned along its diagonal. It stuck out like the broken stub of a tooth. All the rest—the field, the houses, the pines, the forest clearing, the cemetery, the station, the church dating back to Ivan the Terrible, the thin twisting trickle of water from the spring, all the people we knew and those we didn't—everything had ceased to exist, everything had changed its form. Rippling ash stretched away on all sides right to the deserted horizon, along whose grey edge there swayed the saffron caps of chanterelles and flowers like pairs of minute scales. And beyond the horizon stretched the same emptiness further and further to eternity, and then beyond. And from the colourless, and in fact non-existent, sky there fell a strange, invisible, intangible substance, the product of disintegration. Our clothes and our hair also turned to nothing and fell like intangible particles of dry mist, while we slowly and painlessly, like a ball of motheaten wool, began to unwind and unwind, turning into nothing.

We were not at all afraid, but infinitely sad.

'Let's go back,' my wife managed to say, having become completely transparent, diffuse and motionless, like a dream or rather like the memory of a dream. Melting and losing substance before my eyes, she pressed up against my shoulder and I realised that we would not be going back anywhere, because I could not remember the name of that evergreen plant which was covered in the middle of winter with very bright rosy flowers. Only that name could save us. Beyond the grey shroud of the sky, flying into the vastness of the world, silently raging and licking the universe on all sides, was an eerie flame of decaying matter, invisible, intangible, cold and at the same time spreading the sharp unpleasant fresh smell of rust, the smell of oxygen which, it turns out, I had been breathing for some time through rubber tubes inserted deep into my nostrils. I could hear the oxygen bubbles whispering through the gauze over my lips, and I realised fairly clearly that I was no longer asleep but that I was lying in a high surgical bed in my ward, that the black blood dripping into the bottle was my own blood, that outside, under the window, the garden of my heart was in flower, that the slit-eyed anaesthetist had not forgotten to wake me up, that man cannot die until he has been born, nor be born without having died; and that not far away, beside the Holy Well, most likely just as before, the familiar old man was standing and patiently washing his bottles.

why does
this image
remain?